STRATFORD ZOO

MIDNIGHT REVUE PRESENTS:
ROMEO and JULIET

Written by Ian Lendler
Art by Zack Giallongo
Colors by Alisa Harris

:01

First Second
New York

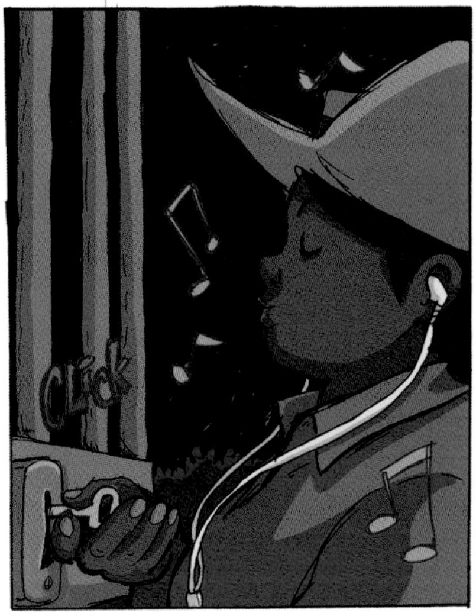
CLICK

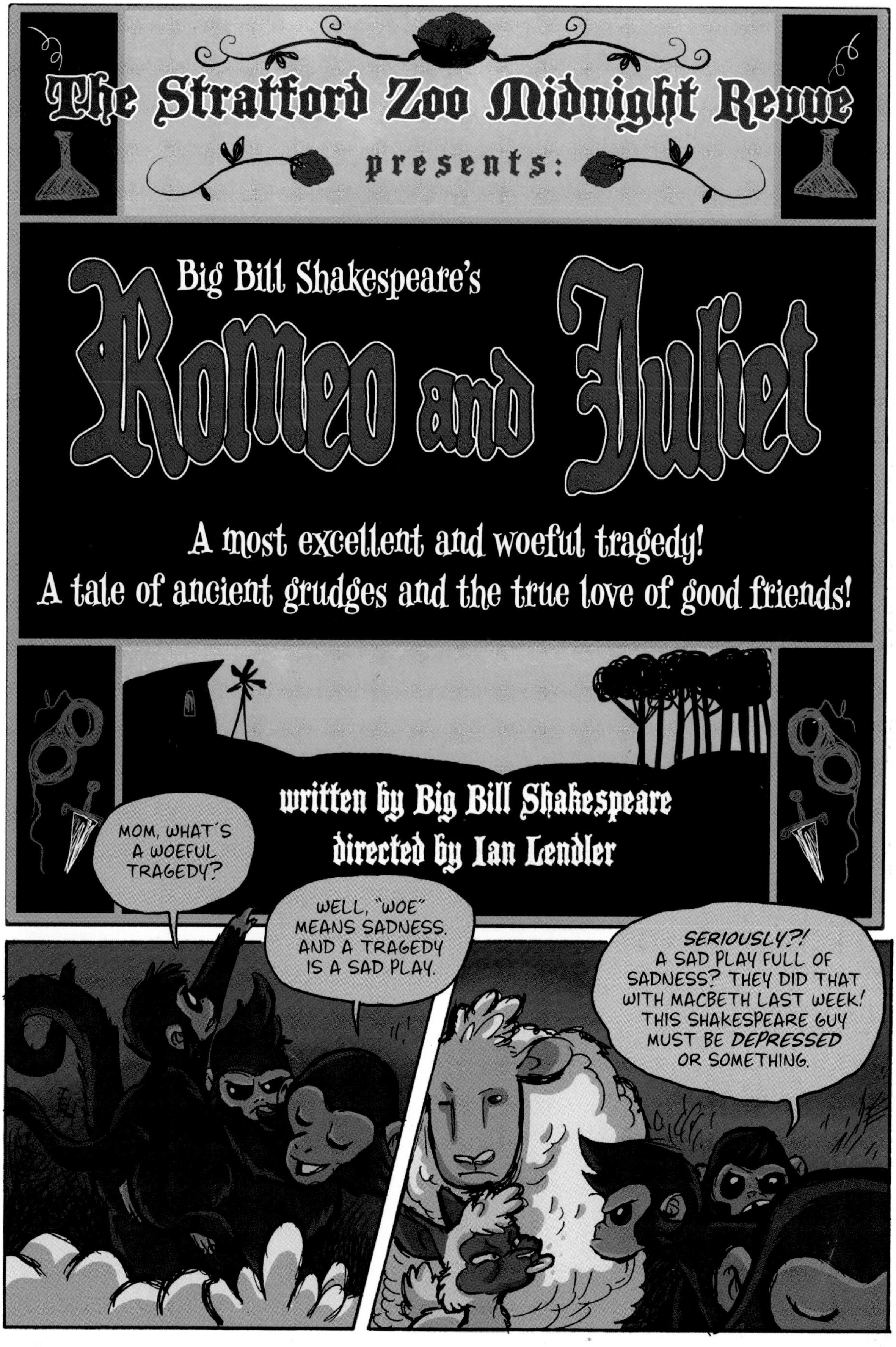
The Stratford Zoo Midnight Revue
presents:
Big Bill Shakespeare's
Romeo and Juliet
A most excellent and woeful tragedy!
A tale of ancient grudges and the true love of good friends!
written by Big Bill Shakespeare
directed by Ian Lendler
MOM, WHAT'S A WOEFUL TRAGEDY?
WELL, "WOE" MEANS SADNESS. AND A TRAGEDY IS A SAD PLAY.
SERIOUSLY?! A SAD PLAY FULL OF SADNESS? THEY DID THAT WITH MACBETH LAST WEEK! THIS SHAKESPEARE GUY MUST BE DEPRESSED OR SOMETHING.

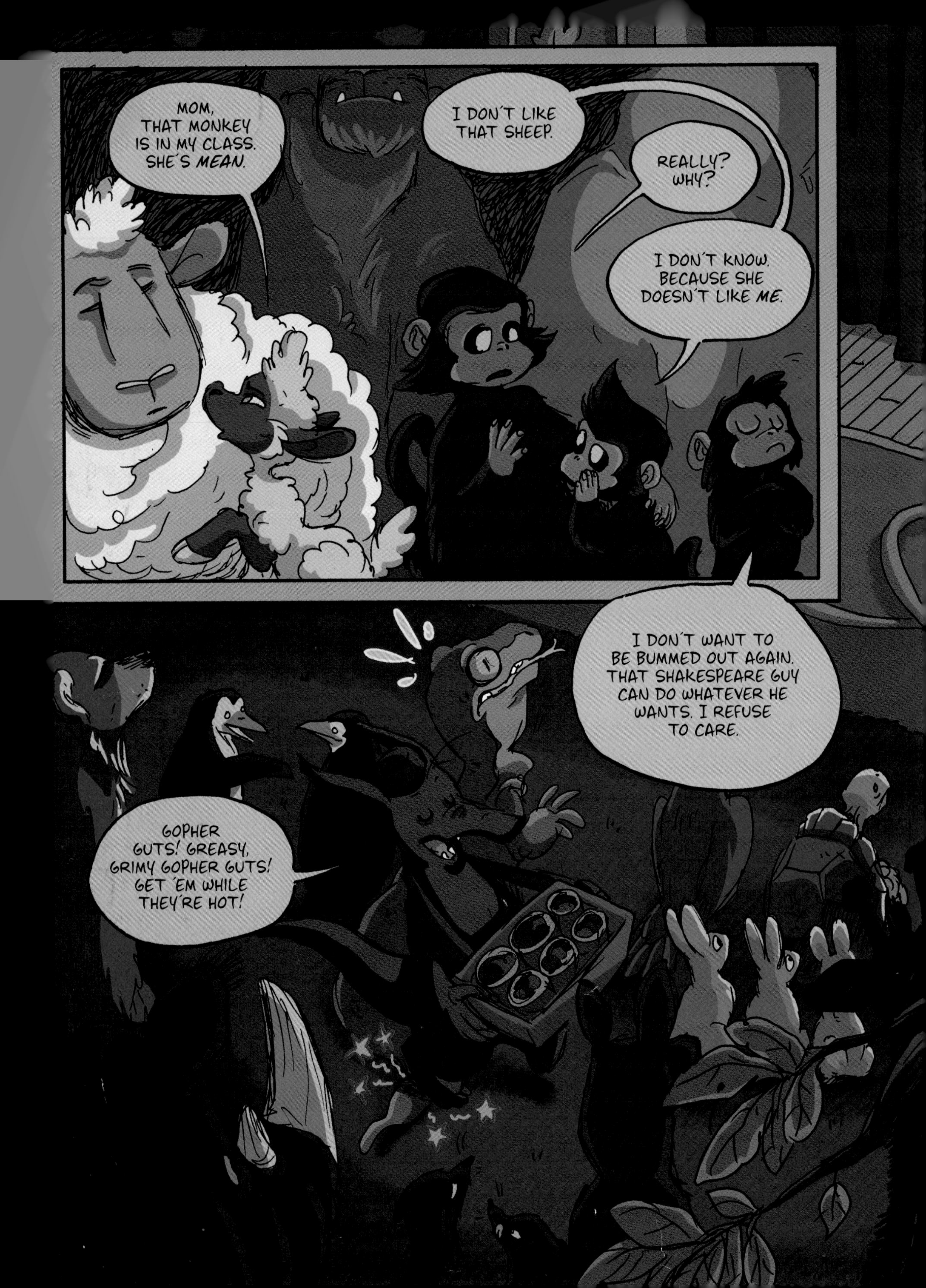
MOM, THAT MONKEY IS IN MY CLASS. SHE'S *MEAN*.
I DON'T LIKE THAT SHEEP.
REALLY? WHY?
I DON'T KNOW. BECAUSE SHE DOESN'T LIKE *ME*.
I DON'T WANT TO BE BUMMED OUT AGAIN. THAT SHAKESPEARE GUY CAN DO WHATEVER HE WANTS. I REFUSE TO CARE.
GOPHER GUTS! GREASY, GRIMY GOPHER GUTS! GET 'EM WHILE THEY'RE HOT!

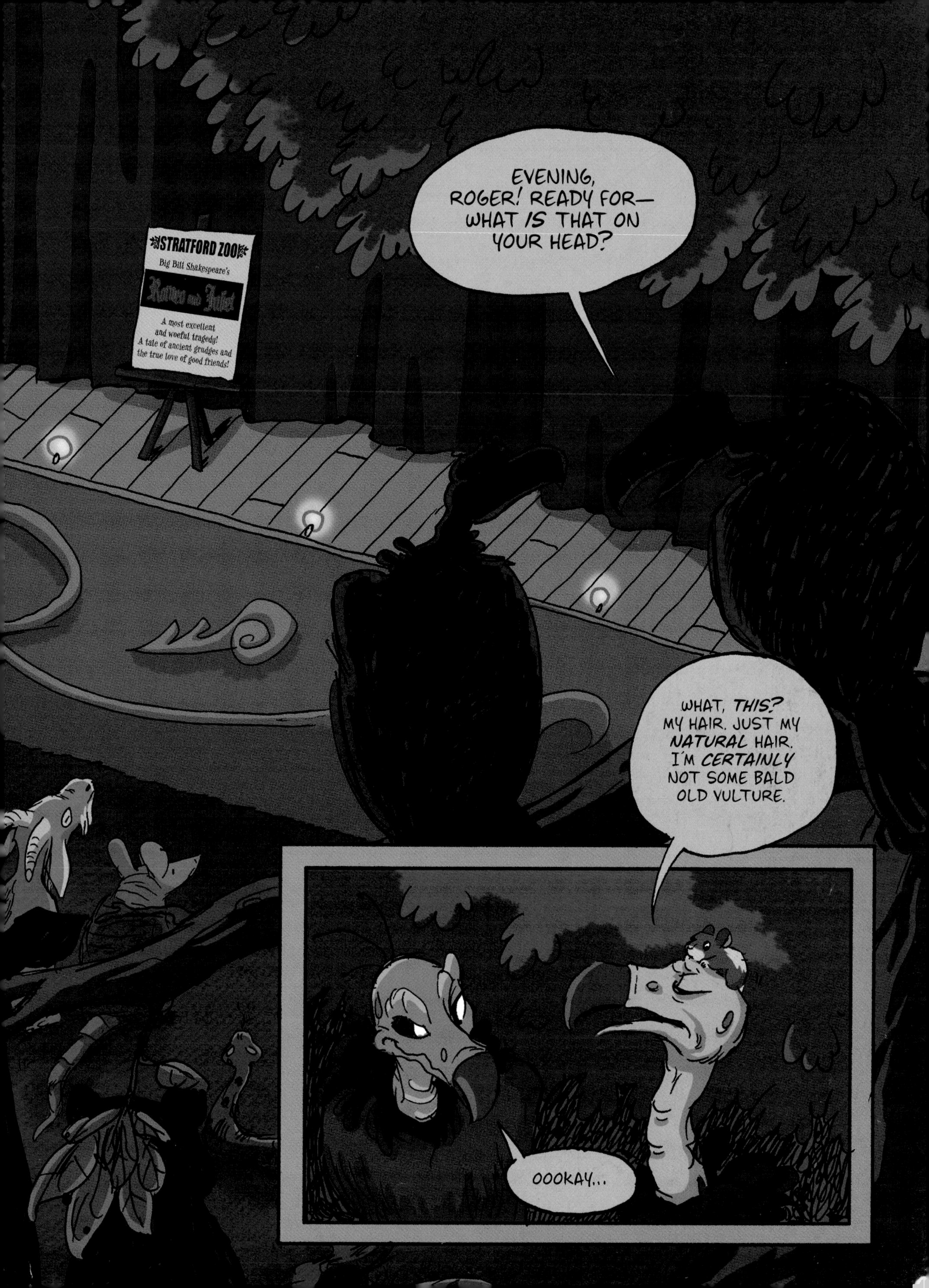
STRATFORD ZOO
Big Bill Shakespeare's
A most excellent and woeful tragedy! A tale of ancient grudges and the true love of good friends!
EVENING, ROGER! READY FOR— WHAT *IS* THAT ON YOUR HEAD?
WHAT, *THIS?* MY HAIR. JUST MY *NATURAL* HAIR. I'M *CERTAINLY* NOT SOME BALD OLD VULTURE.
OOOKAY...

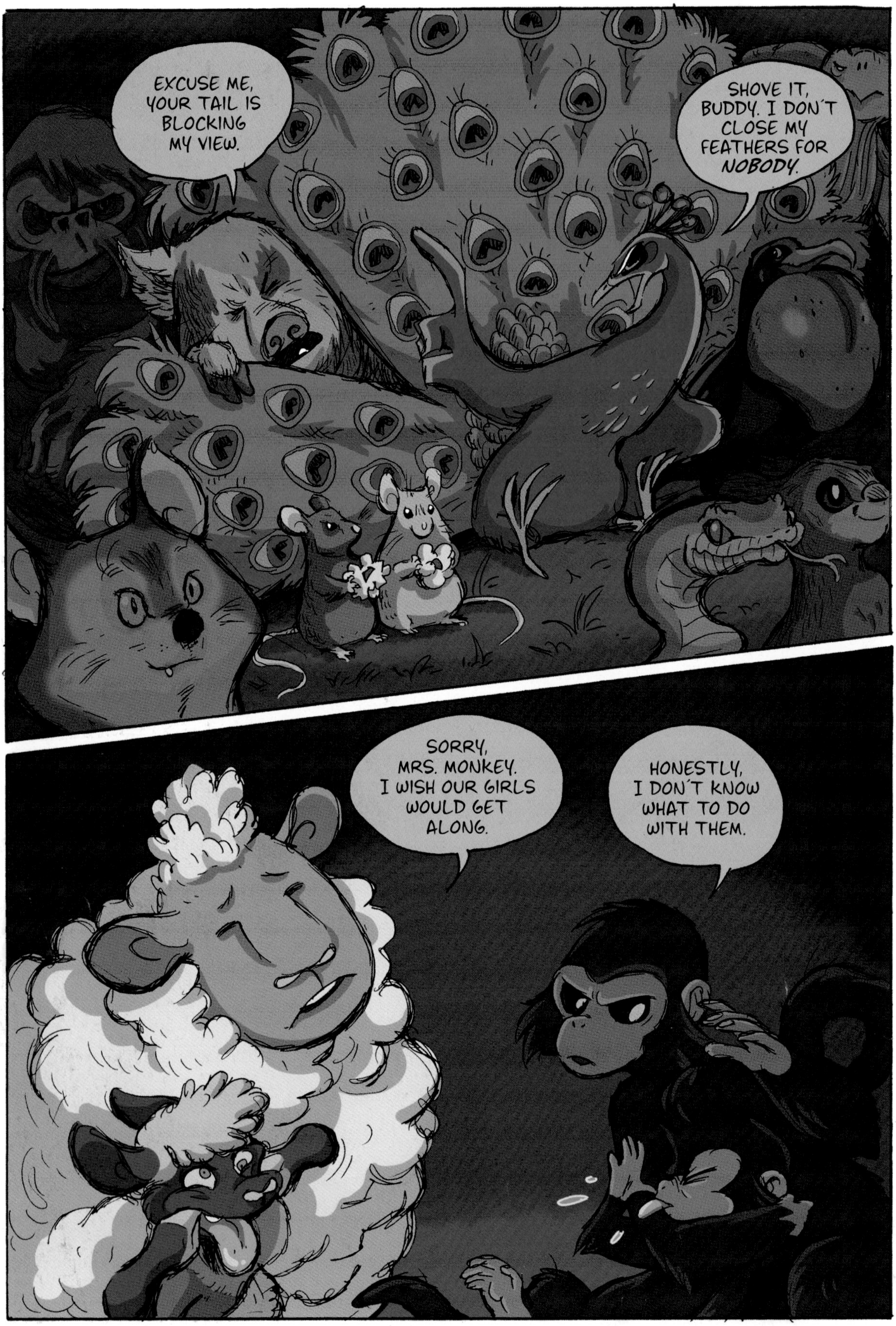
EXCUSE ME, YOUR TAIL IS BLOCKING MY VIEW.
SHOVE IT, BUDDY. I DON'T CLOSE MY FEATHERS FOR *NOBODY*.
SORRY, MRS. MONKEY. I WISH OUR GIRLS WOULD GET ALONG.
HONESTLY, I DON'T KNOW WHAT TO DO WITH THEM.

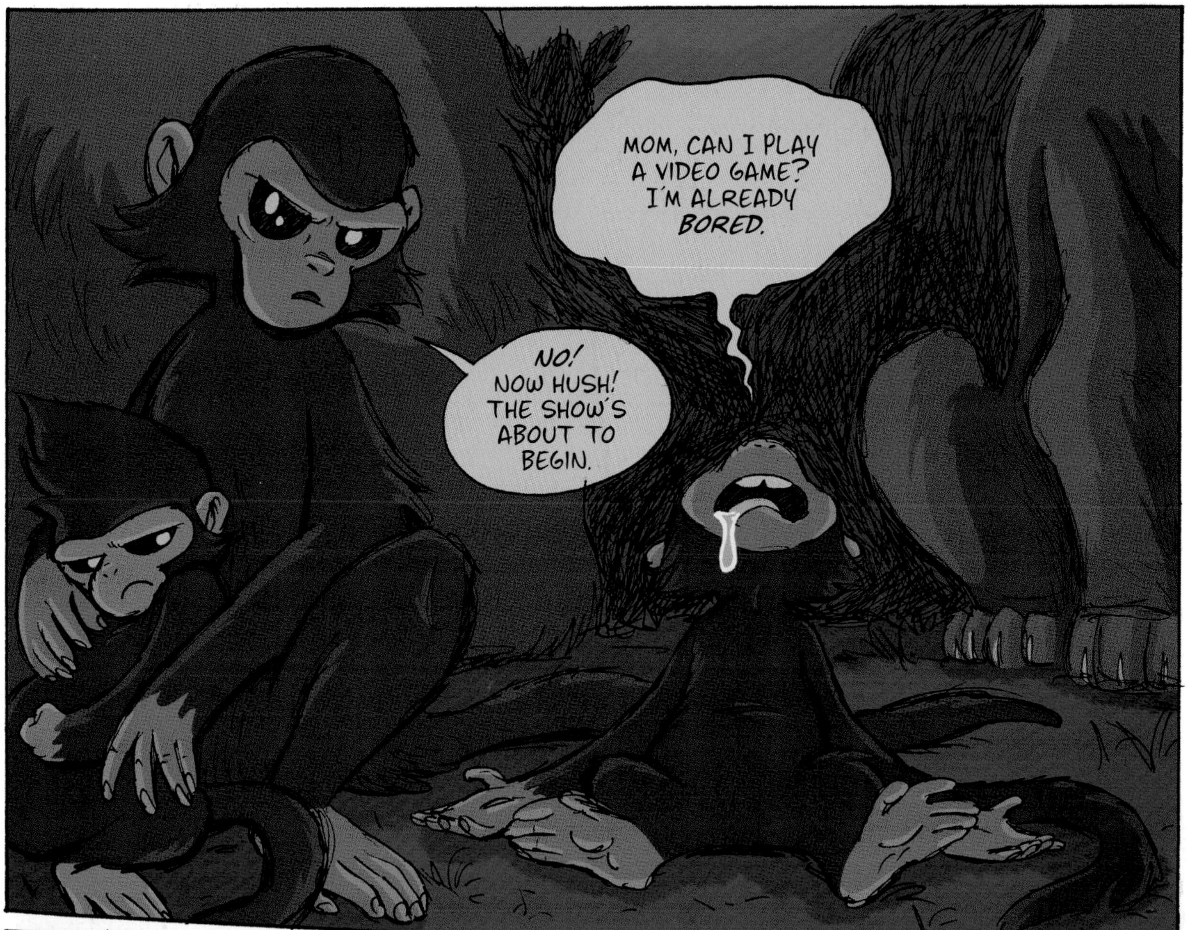
MOM, CAN I PLAY A VIDEO GAME? I'M ALREADY *BORED.*
NO! NOW HUSH! THE SHOW'S ABOUT TO BEGIN.

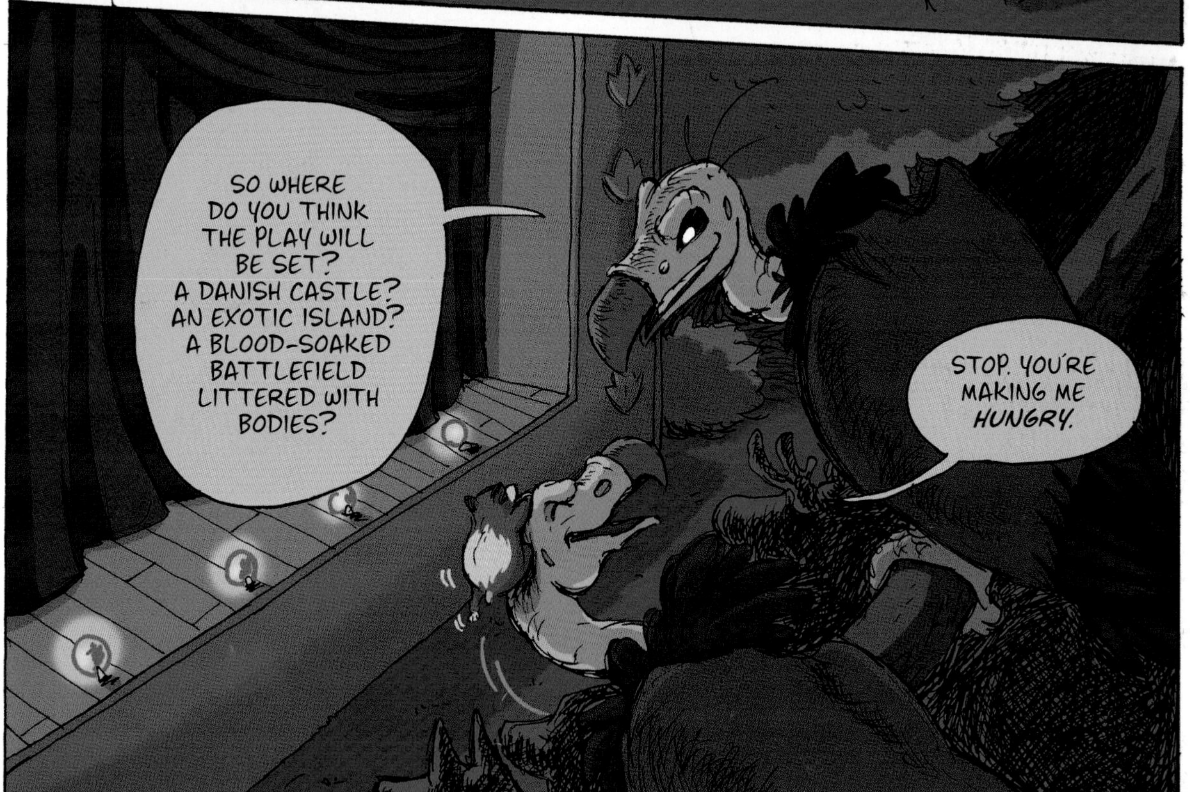
SO WHERE DO YOU THINK THE PLAY WILL BE SET? A DANISH CASTLE? AN EXOTIC ISLAND? A BLOOD-SOAKED BATTLEFIELD LITTERED WITH BODIES?
STOP. YOU'RE MAKING ME *HUNGRY.*

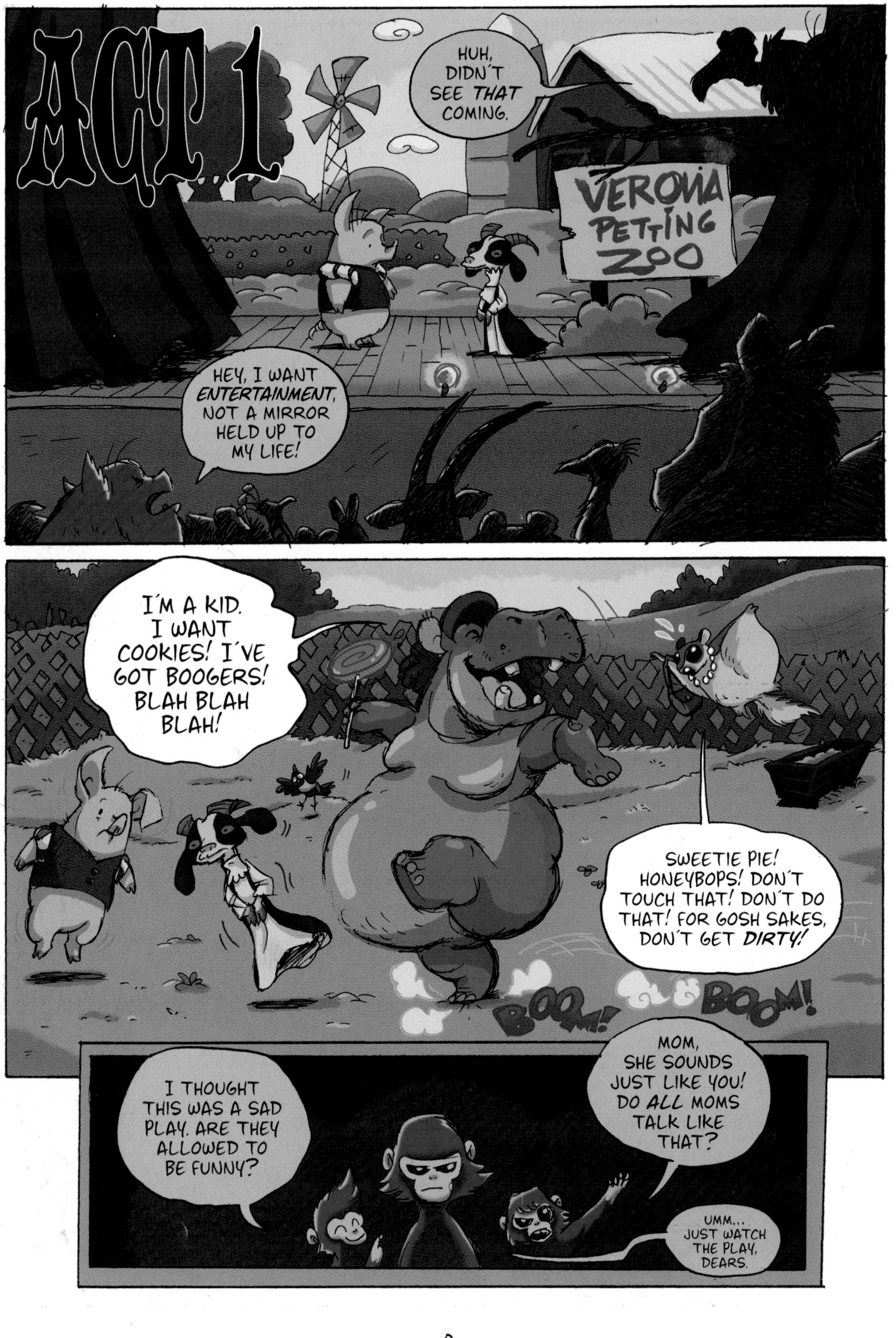
ACT 1
HUH, DIDN'T SEE THAT COMING.
VERONA PETTING ZOO
HEY, I WANT ENTERTAINMENT, NOT A MIRROR HELD UP TO MY LIFE!
I'M A KID. I WANT COOKIES! I'VE GOT BOOGERS! BLAH BLAH BLAH!
SWEETIE PIE! HONEYBOPS! DON'T TOUCH THAT! DON'T DO THAT! FOR GOSH SAKES, DON'T GET DIRTY!
BOOM! BOOM!
I THOUGHT THIS WAS A SAD PLAY. ARE THEY ALLOWED TO BE FUNNY?
MOM, SHE SOUNDS JUST LIKE YOU! DO ALL MOMS TALK LIKE THAT?
UMM... JUST WATCH THE PLAY, DEARS.

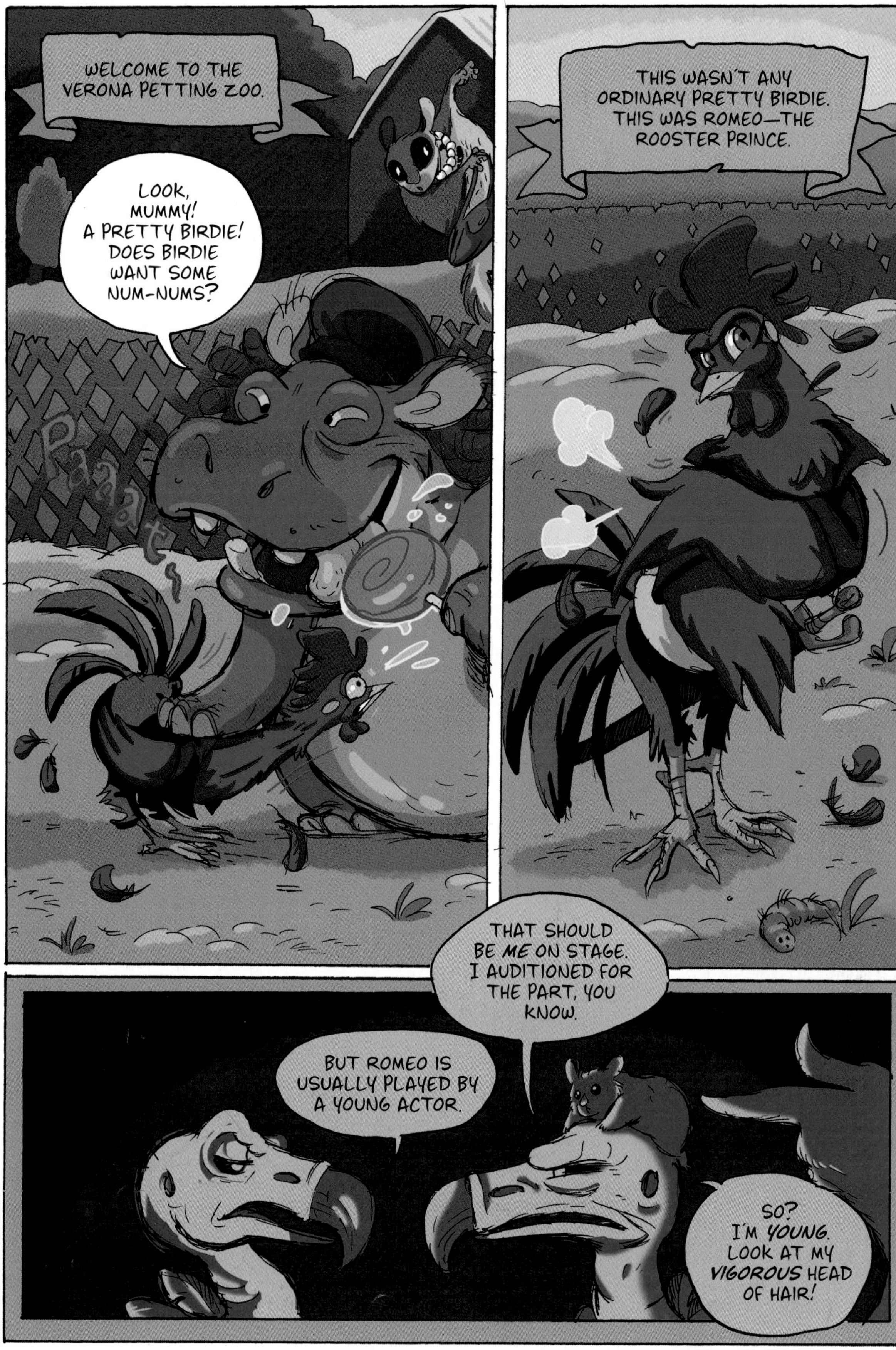

WELCOME TO THE VERONA PETTING ZOO.
LOOK, MUMMY! A PRETTY BIRDIE! DOES BIRDIE WANT SOME NUM-NUMS?
Paaaat
THIS WASN'T ANY ORDINARY PRETTY BIRDIE. THIS WAS ROMEO—THE ROOSTER PRINCE.
THAT SHOULD BE *ME* ON STAGE. I AUDITIONED FOR THE PART, YOU KNOW.
BUT ROMEO IS USUALLY PLAYED BY A YOUNG ACTOR.
SO? I'M *YOUNG*. LOOK AT MY *VIGOROUS* HEAD OF HAIR!

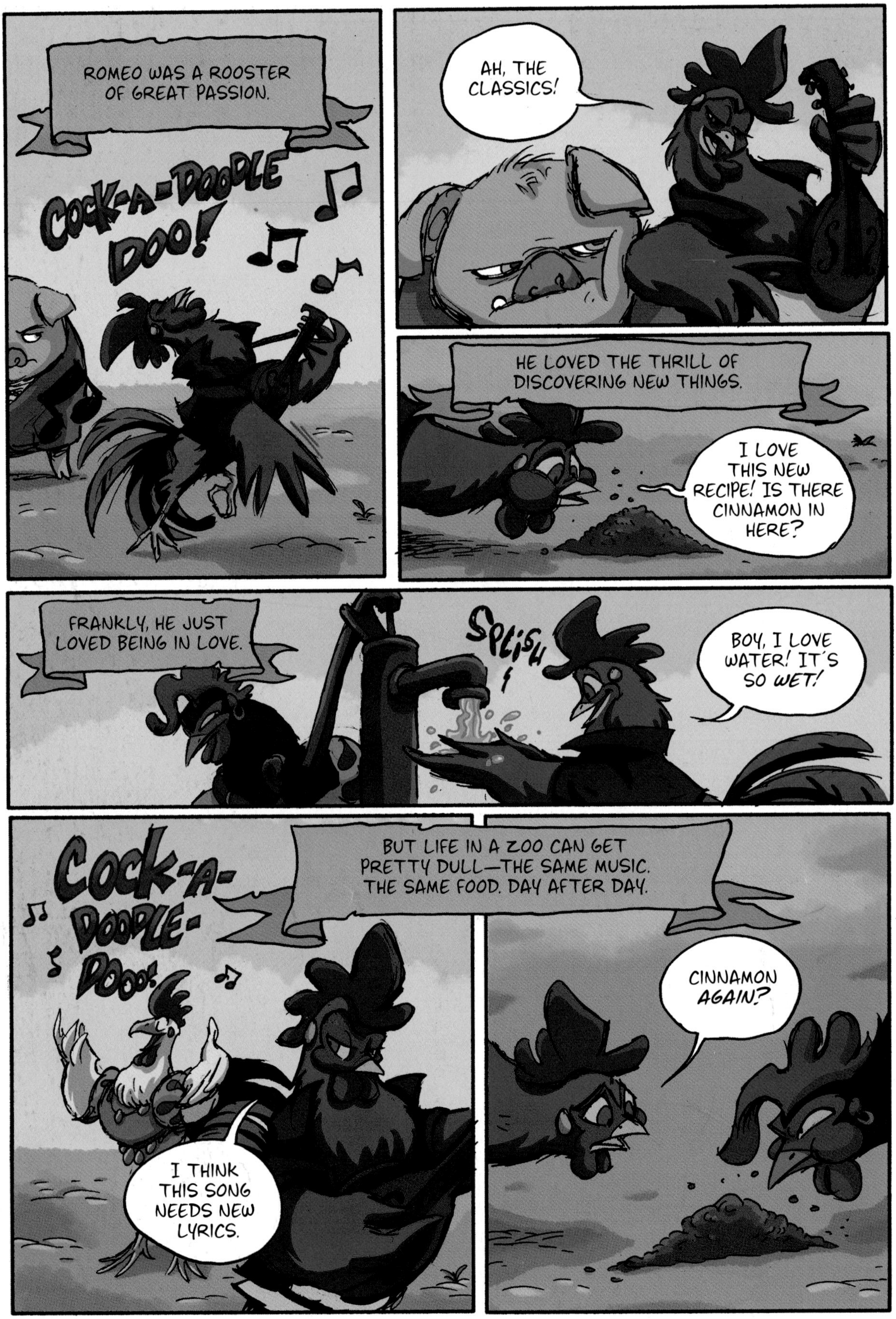

ROMEO WAS A ROOSTER OF GREAT PASSION.
COCK-A-DOODLE DOO!
AH, THE CLASSICS!
HE LOVED THE THRILL OF DISCOVERING NEW THINGS.
I LOVE THIS NEW RECIPE! IS THERE CINNAMON IN HERE?
FRANKLY, HE JUST LOVED BEING IN LOVE.
SPLISH
BOY, I LOVE WATER! IT'S SO WET!
BUT LIFE IN A ZOO CAN GET PRETTY DULL—THE SAME MUSIC. THE SAME FOOD. DAY AFTER DAY.
COCK-A-DOODLE-DOOO!
I THINK THIS SONG NEEDS NEW LYRICS.
CINNAMON AGAIN?

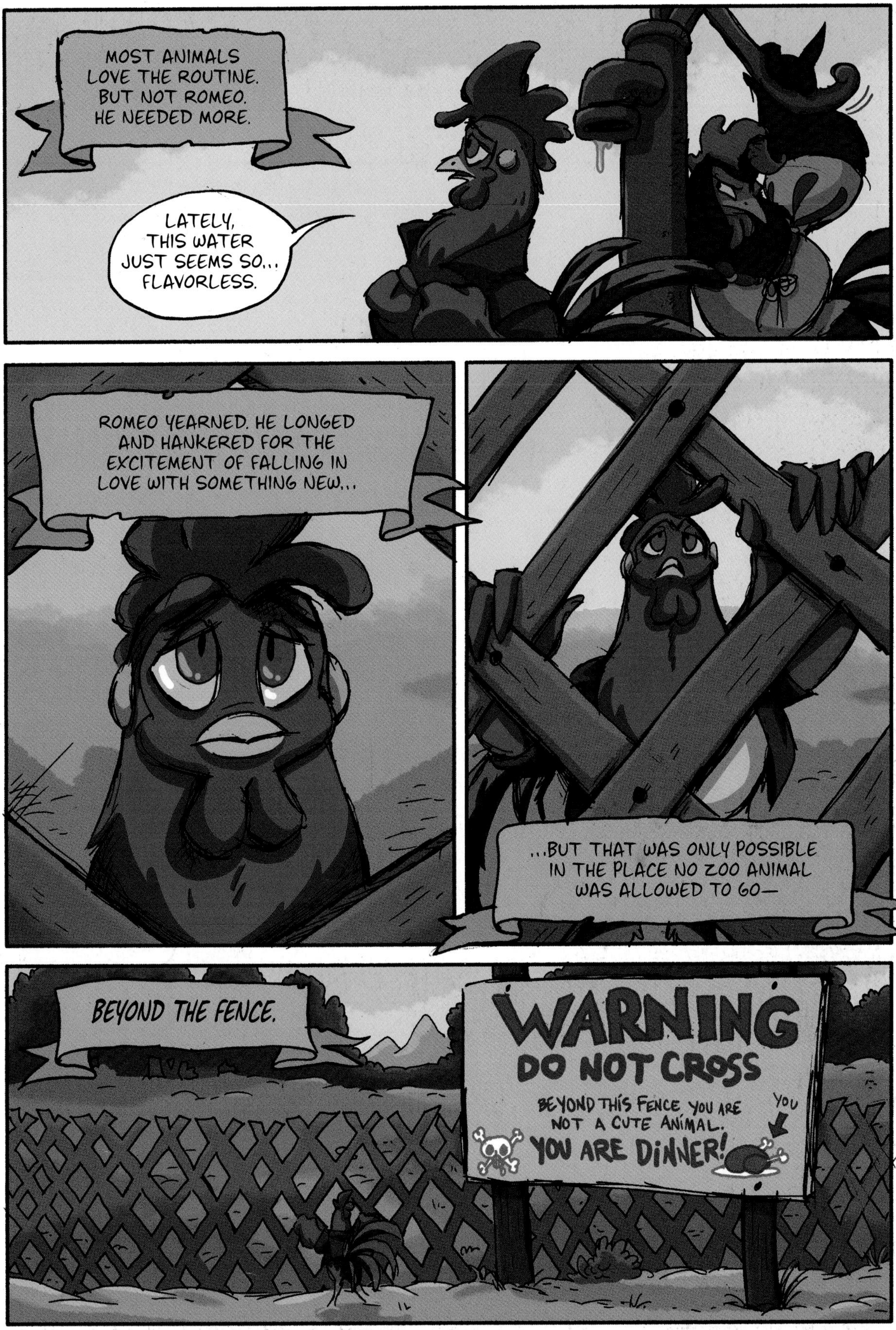
MOST ANIMALS LOVE THE ROUTINE. BUT NOT ROMEO. HE NEEDED MORE.
LATELY, THIS WATER JUST SEEMS SO... FLAVORLESS.
ROMEO YEARNED. HE LONGED AND HANKERED FOR THE EXCITEMENT OF FALLING IN LOVE WITH SOMETHING NEW...
...BUT THAT WAS ONLY POSSIBLE IN THE PLACE NO ZOO ANIMAL WAS ALLOWED TO GO—
BEYOND THE FENCE.
WARNING
DO NOT CROSS
BEYOND THIS FENCE YOU ARE NOT A CUTE ANIMAL.
YOU ARE DINNER!
YOU

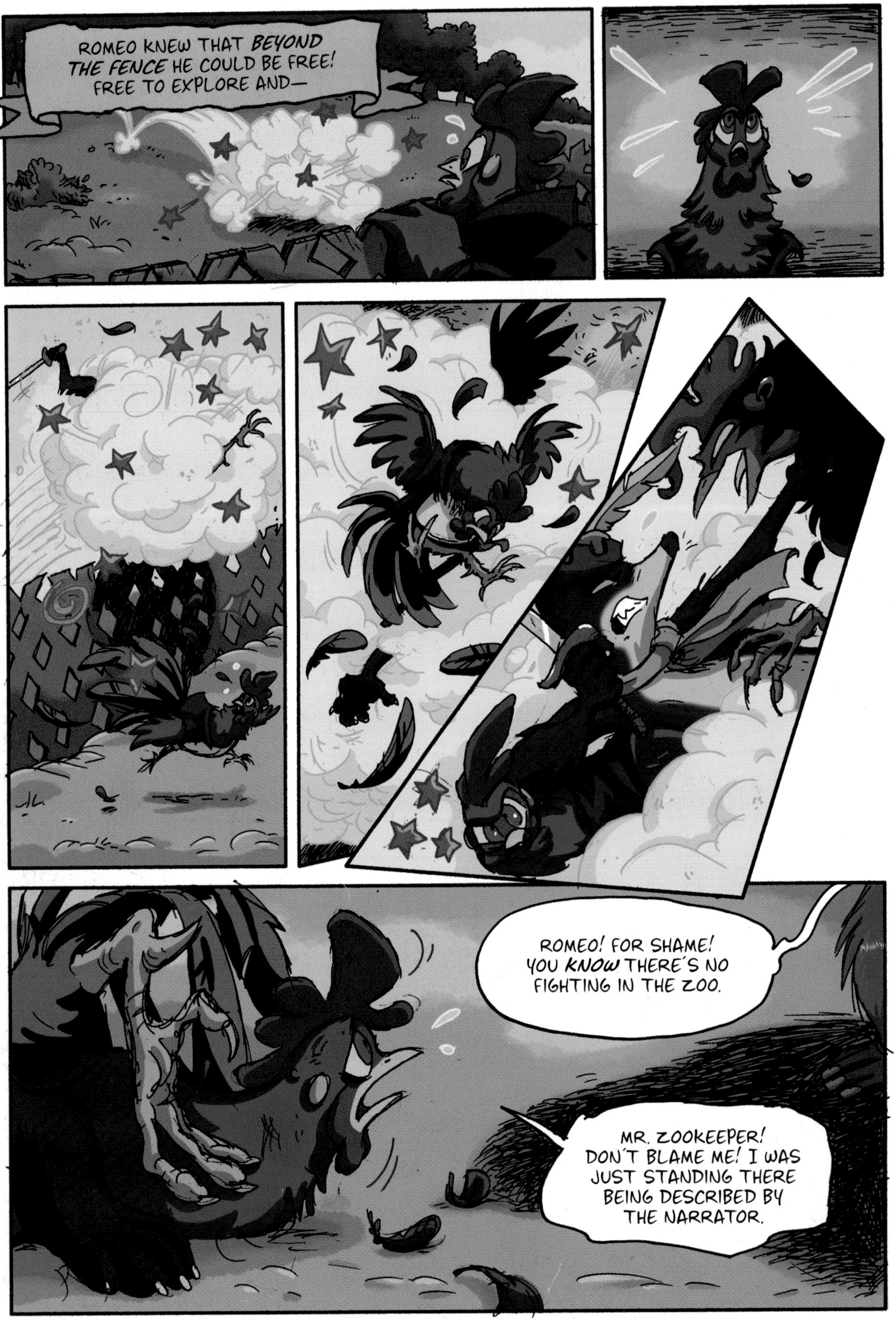
ROMEO KNEW THAT *BEYOND THE FENCE* HE COULD BE FREE! FREE TO EXPLORE AND—
ROMEO! FOR SHAME! YOU *KNOW* THERE'S NO FIGHTING IN THE ZOO.
MR. ZOOKEEPER! DON'T BLAME ME! I WAS JUST STANDING THERE BEING DESCRIBED BY THE NARRATOR.

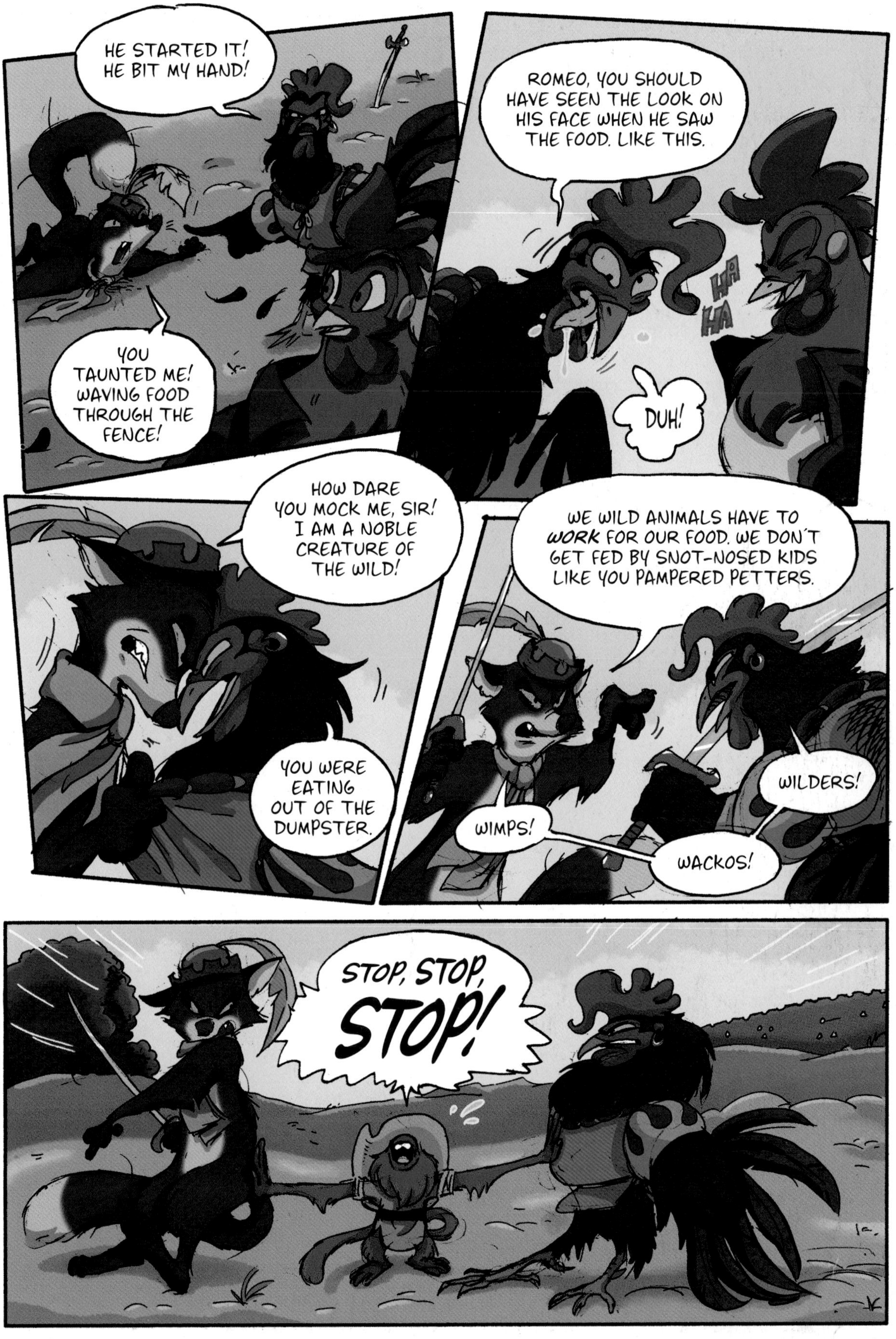
HE STARTED IT! HE BIT MY HAND!
YOU TAUNTED ME! WAVING FOOD THROUGH THE FENCE!
ROMEO, YOU SHOULD HAVE SEEN THE LOOK ON HIS FACE WHEN HE SAW THE FOOD. LIKE THIS.
DUH!
HA HA
HOW DARE YOU MOCK ME, SIR! I AM A NOBLE CREATURE OF THE WILD!
YOU WERE EATING OUT OF THE DUMPSTER.
WE WILD ANIMALS HAVE TO WORK FOR OUR FOOD. WE DON'T GET FED BY SNOT-NOSED KIDS LIKE YOU PAMPERED PETTERS.
WILDERS!
WIMPS!
WACKOS!
STOP, STOP, STOP!

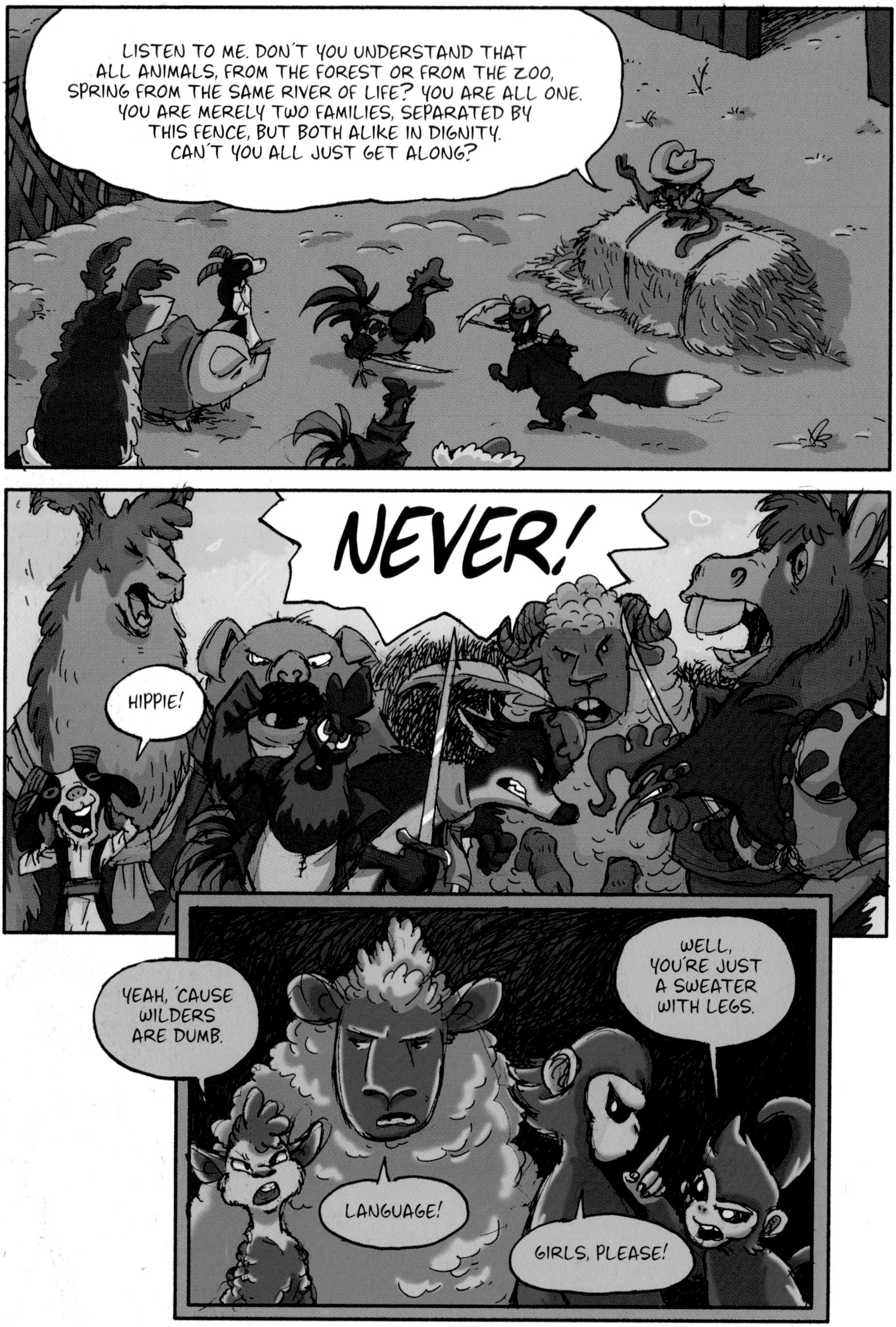
LISTEN TO ME. DON´T YOU UNDERSTAND THAT ALL ANIMALS, FROM THE FOREST OR FROM THE ZOO, SPRING FROM THE SAME RIVER OF LIFE? YOU ARE ALL ONE. YOU ARE MERELY TWO FAMILIES, SEPARATED BY THIS FENCE, BUT BOTH ALIKE IN DIGNITY. CAN´T YOU ALL JUST GET ALONG?
NEVER!
HIPPIE!
YEAH, ´CAUSE WILDERS ARE DUMB.
WELL, YOU´RE JUST A SWEATER WITH LEGS.
LANGUAGE!
GIRLS, PLEASE!

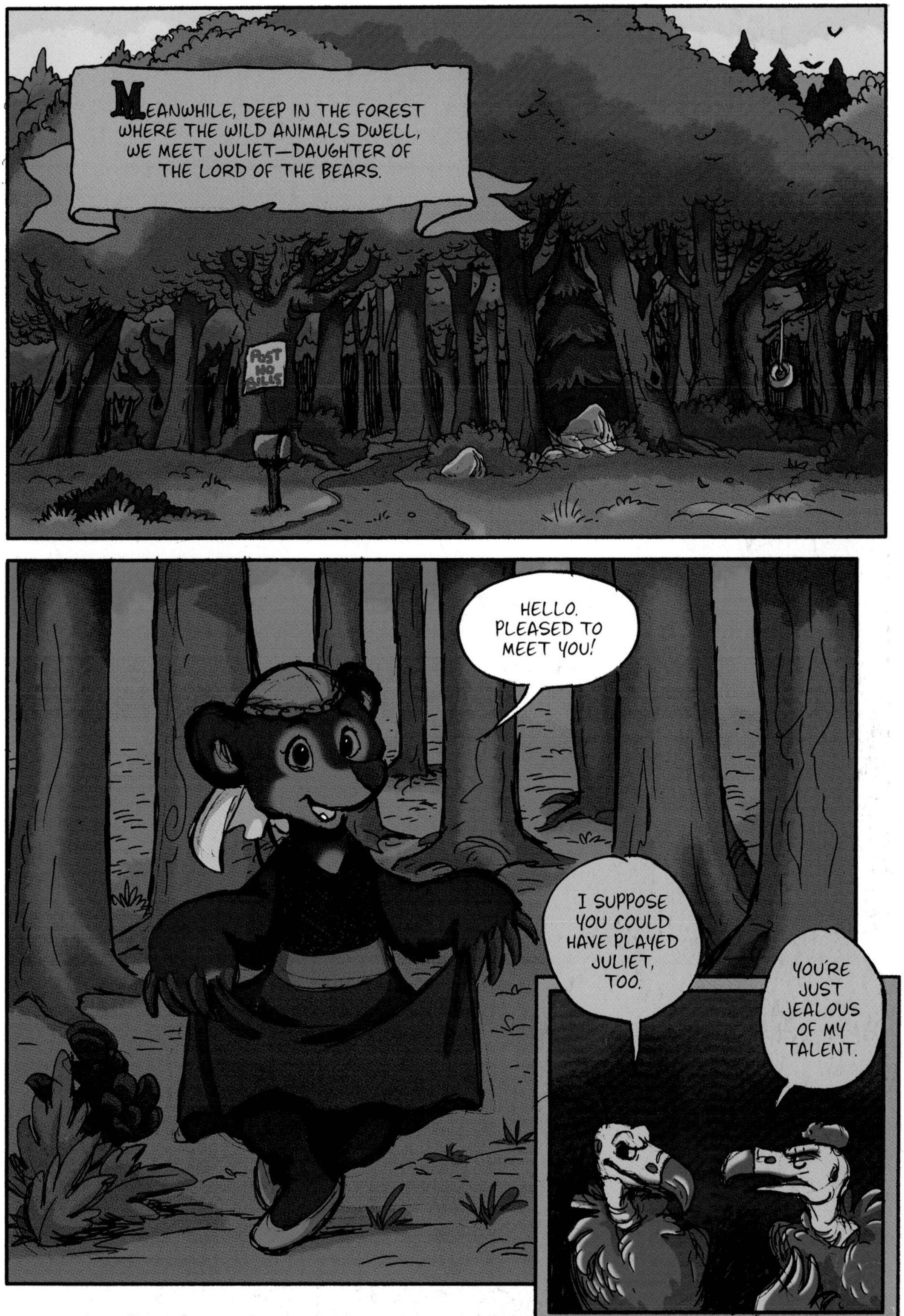
MEANWHILE, DEEP IN THE FOREST WHERE THE WILD ANIMALS DWELL, WE MEET JULIET—DAUGHTER OF THE LORD OF THE BEARS.
POST NO BILLS
HELLO. PLEASED TO MEET YOU!
I SUPPOSE YOU COULD HAVE PLAYED JULIET, TOO.
YOU'RE JUST JEALOUS OF MY TALENT.

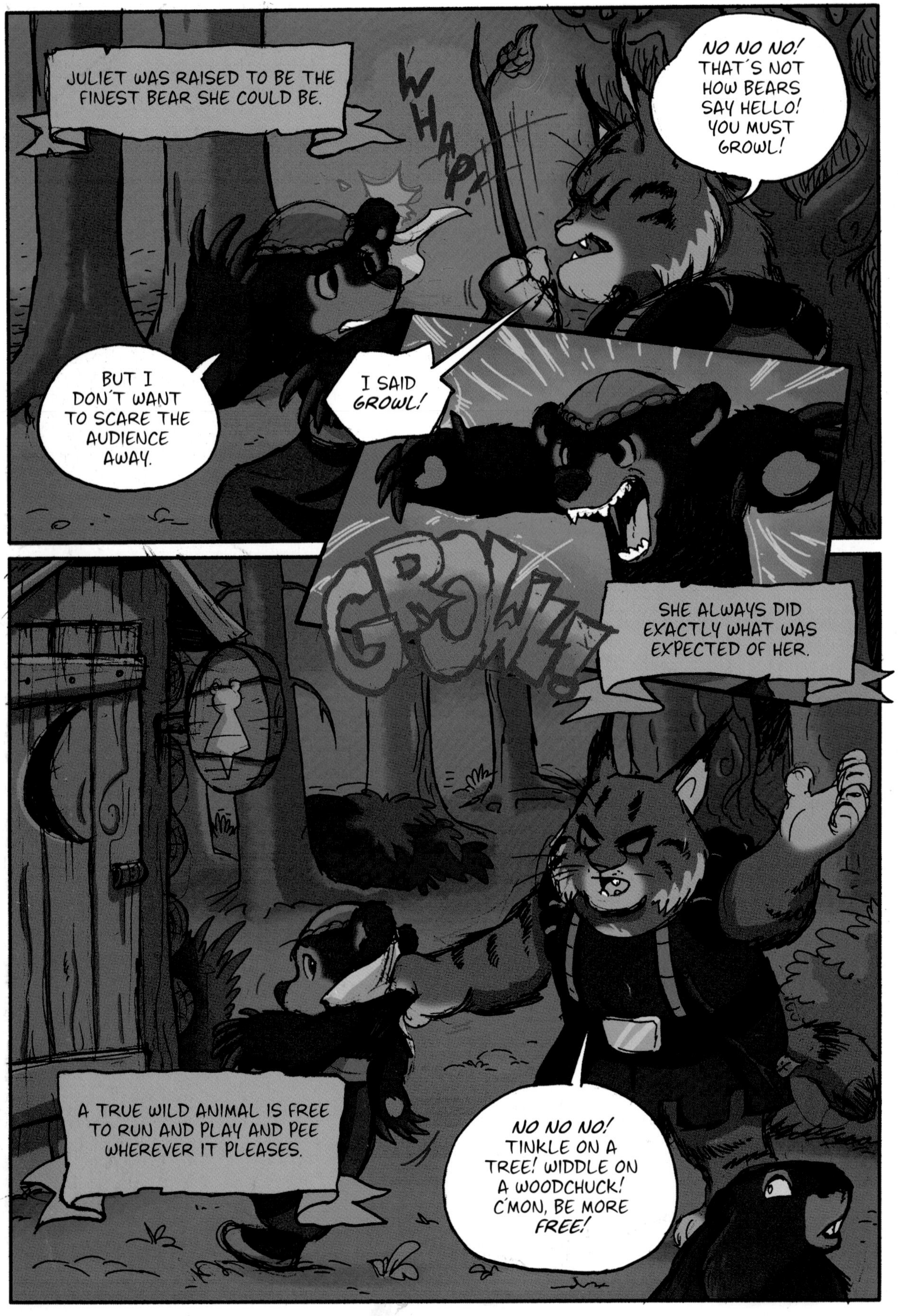

JULIET WAS RAISED TO BE THE FINEST BEAR SHE COULD BE.
WHAP!
NO NO NO! THAT'S NOT HOW BEARS SAY HELLO! YOU MUST GROWL!
BUT I DON'T WANT TO SCARE THE AUDIENCE AWAY.
I SAID GROWL!
GROWL!
SHE ALWAYS DID EXACTLY WHAT WAS EXPECTED OF HER.
A TRUE WILD ANIMAL IS FREE TO RUN AND PLAY AND PEE WHEREVER IT PLEASES.
NO NO NO! TINKLE ON A TREE! WIDDLE ON A WOODCHUCK! C'MON, BE MORE FREE!

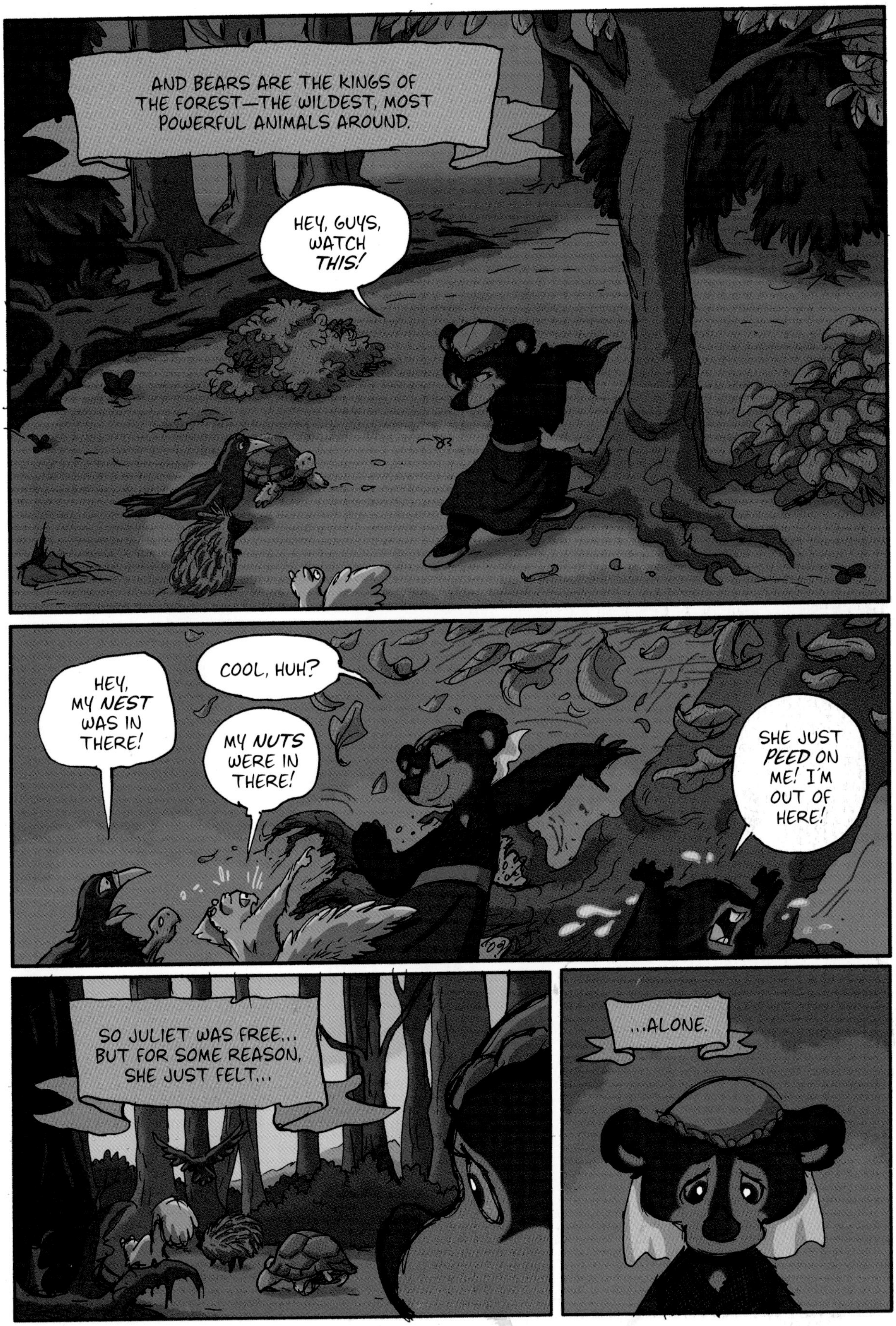
AND BEARS ARE THE KINGS OF THE FOREST—THE WILDEST, MOST POWERFUL ANIMALS AROUND.
HEY, GUYS, WATCH THIS!
HEY, MY NEST WAS IN THERE!
COOL, HUH?
MY NUTS WERE IN THERE!
SHE JUST PEED ON ME! I'M OUT OF HERE!
SO JULIET WAS FREE... BUT FOR SOME REASON, SHE JUST FELT...
...ALONE.

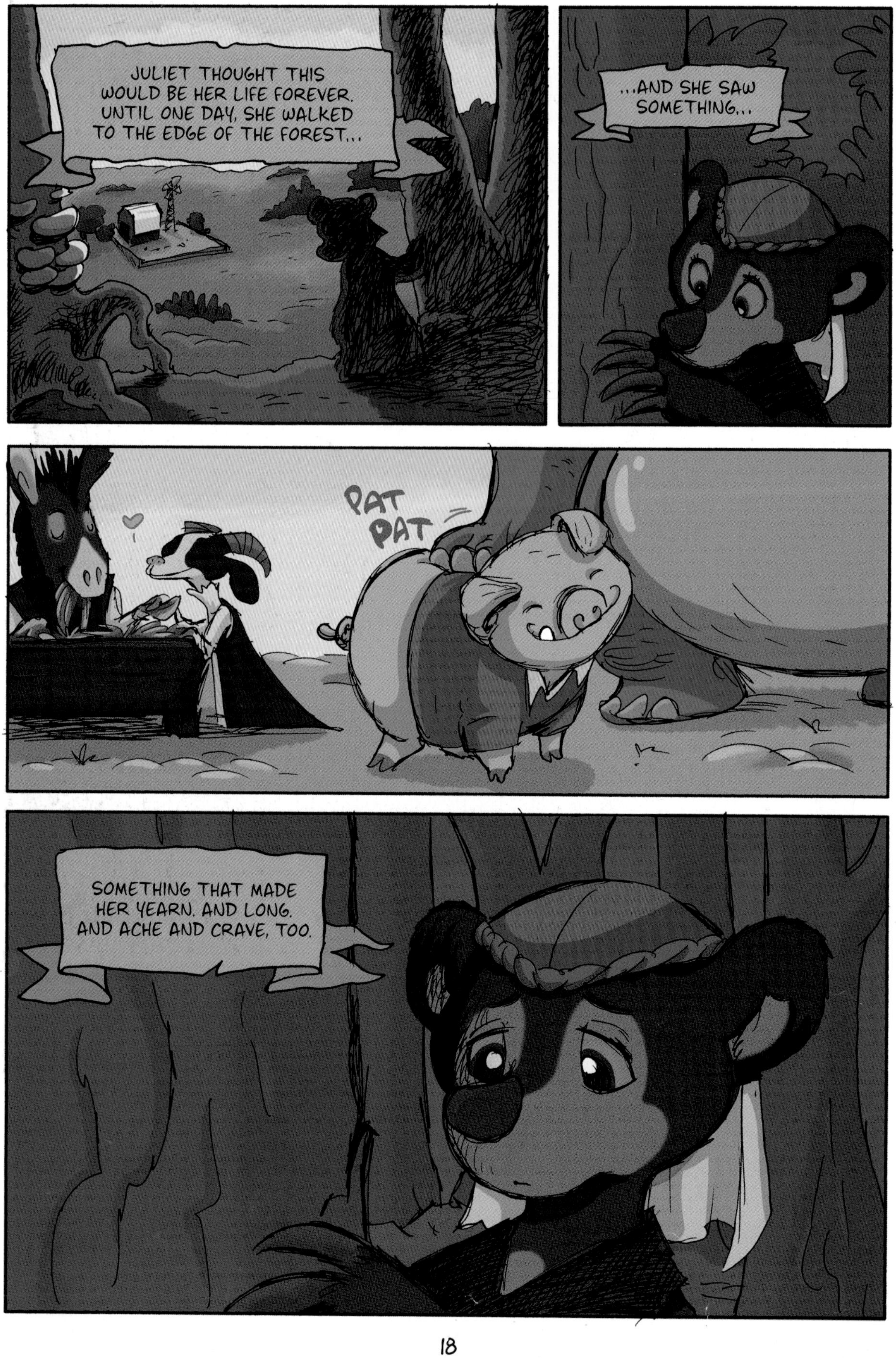
JULIET THOUGHT THIS WOULD BE HER LIFE FOREVER. UNTIL ONE DAY, SHE WALKED TO THE EDGE OF THE FOREST...
...AND SHE SAW SOMETHING...
PAT PAT
SOMETHING THAT MADE HER YEARN. AND LONG. AND ACHE AND CRAVE, TOO.

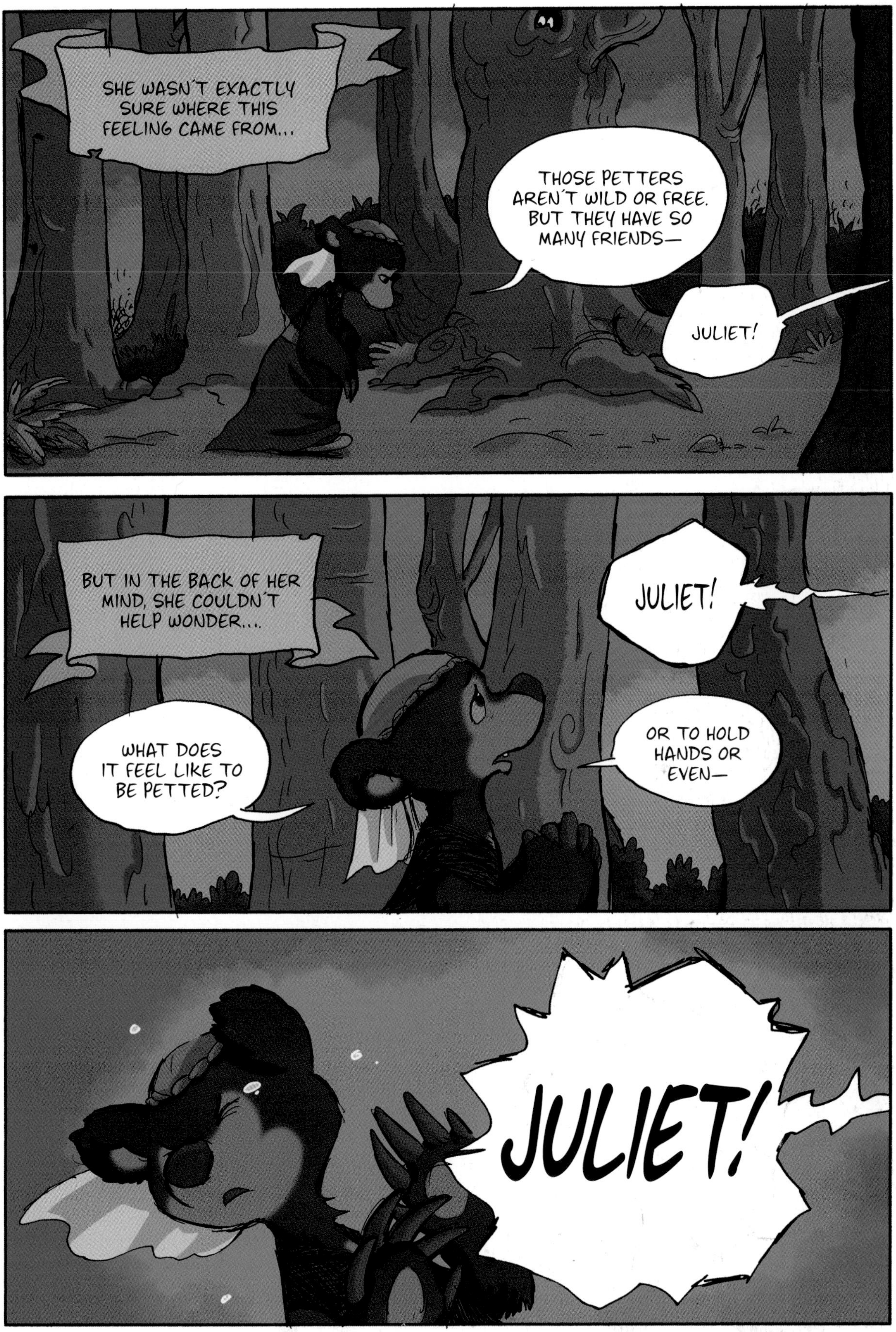
SHE WASN´T EXACTLY SURE WHERE THIS FEELING CAME FROM...
THOSE PETTERS AREN´T WILD OR FREE. BUT THEY HAVE SO MANY FRIENDS—
JULIET!
BUT IN THE BACK OF HER MIND, SHE COULDN´T HELP WONDER...
JULIET!
WHAT DOES IT FEEL LIKE TO BE PETTED?
OR TO HOLD HANDS OR EVEN—
JULIET!

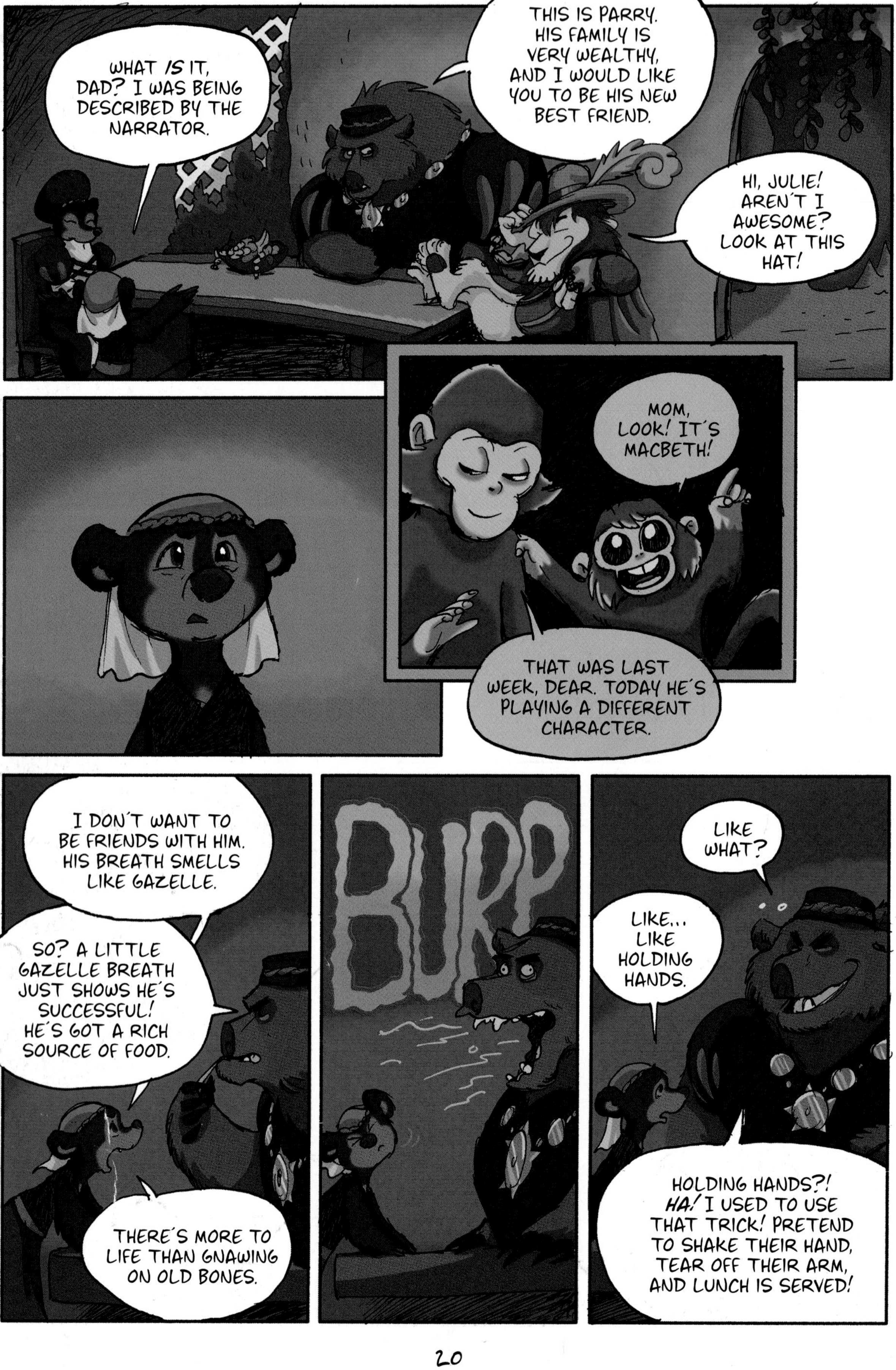
WHAT *IS* IT, DAD? I WAS BEING DESCRIBED BY THE NARRATOR.
THIS IS PARRY. HIS FAMILY IS VERY WEALTHY, AND I WOULD LIKE YOU TO BE HIS NEW BEST FRIEND.
HI, JULIE! AREN'T I AWESOME? LOOK AT THIS HAT!
MOM, LOOK! IT'S MACBETH!
THAT WAS LAST WEEK, DEAR. TODAY HE'S PLAYING A DIFFERENT CHARACTER.
I DON'T WANT TO BE FRIENDS WITH HIM. HIS BREATH SMELLS LIKE GAZELLE.
SO? A LITTLE GAZELLE BREATH JUST SHOWS HE'S SUCCESSFUL! HE'S GOT A RICH SOURCE OF FOOD.
THERE'S MORE TO LIFE THAN GNAWING ON OLD BONES.
BURP
LIKE WHAT?
LIKE... LIKE HOLDING HANDS.
HOLDING HANDS?! *HA!* I USED TO USE THAT TRICK! PRETEND TO SHAKE THEIR HAND, TEAR OFF THEIR ARM, AND LUNCH IS SERVED!

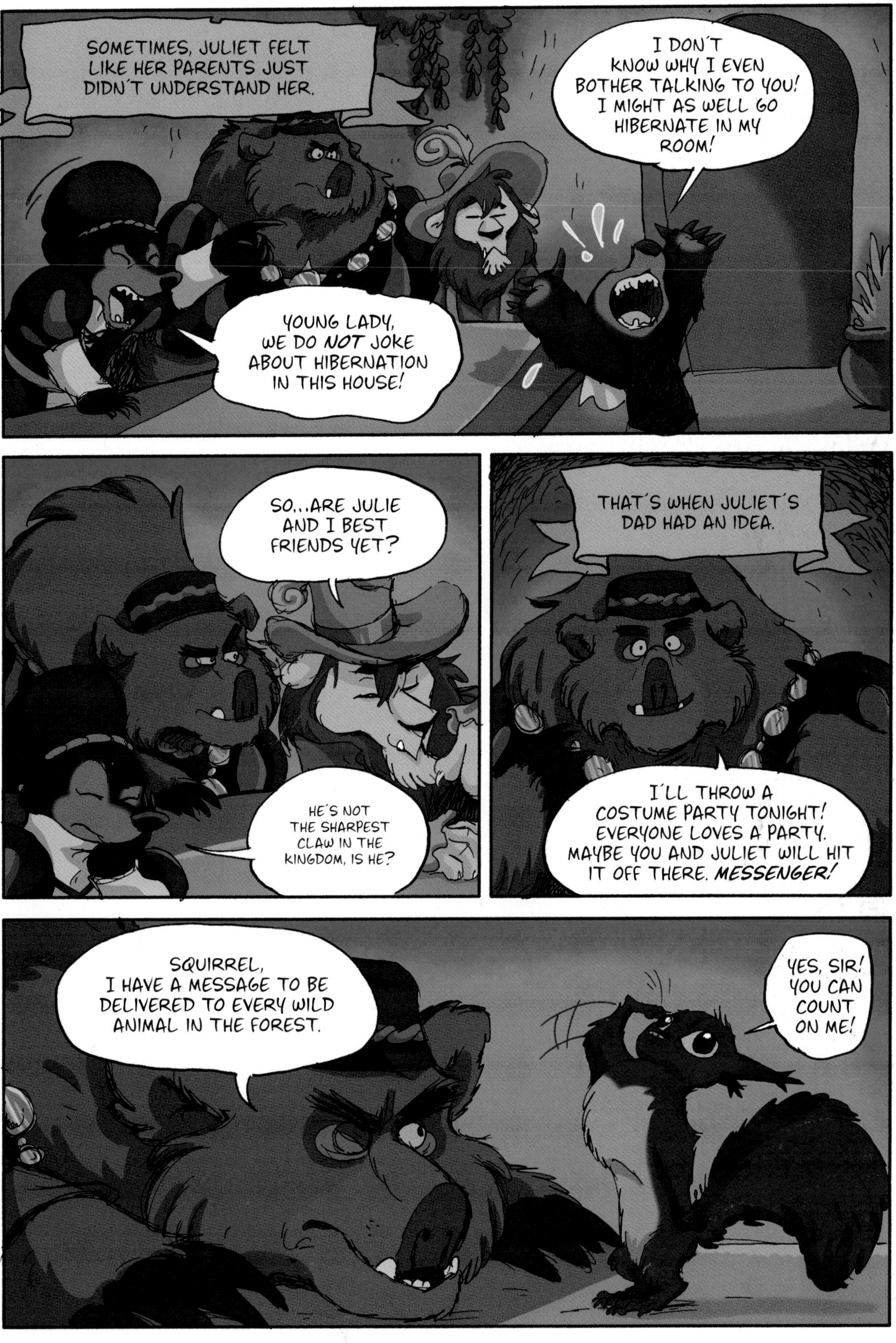
SOMETIMES, JULIET FELT LIKE HER PARENTS JUST DIDN´T UNDERSTAND HER.
I DON´T KNOW WHY I EVEN BOTHER TALKING TO YOU! I MIGHT AS WELL GO HIBERNATE IN MY ROOM!
YOUNG LADY, WE DO *NOT* JOKE ABOUT HIBERNATION IN THIS HOUSE!
SO...ARE JULIE AND I BEST FRIENDS YET?
HE´S NOT THE SHARPEST CLAW IN THE KINGDOM, IS HE?
THAT´S WHEN JULIET´S DAD HAD AN IDEA.
I´LL THROW A COSTUME PARTY TONIGHT! EVERYONE LOVES A PARTY. MAYBE YOU AND JULIET WILL HIT IT OFF THERE. ***MESSENGER!***
SQUIRREL, I HAVE A MESSAGE TO BE DELIVERED TO EVERY WILD ANIMAL IN THE FOREST.
YES, SIR! YOU CAN COUNT ON ME!

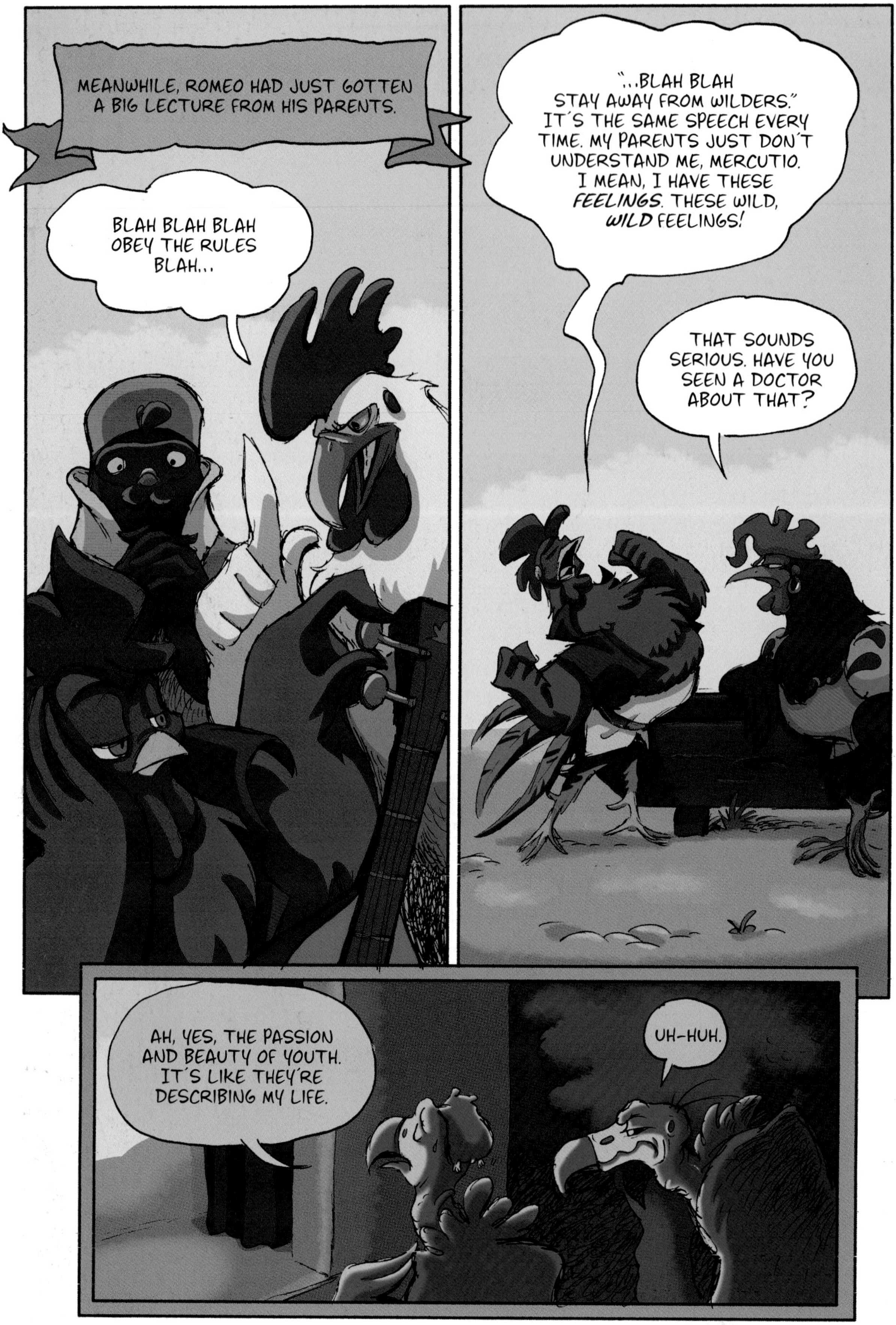
MEANWHILE, ROMEO HAD JUST GOTTEN A BIG LECTURE FROM HIS PARENTS.
BLAH BLAH BLAH OBEY THE RULES BLAH...
"...BLAH BLAH STAY AWAY FROM WILDERS." IT'S THE SAME SPEECH EVERY TIME. MY PARENTS JUST DON'T UNDERSTAND ME, MERCUTIO. I MEAN, I HAVE THESE *FEELINGS*. THESE WILD, *WILD* FEELINGS!
THAT SOUNDS SERIOUS. HAVE YOU SEEN A DOCTOR ABOUT THAT?
AH, YES, THE PASSION AND BEAUTY OF YOUTH. IT'S LIKE THEY'RE DESCRIBING MY LIFE.
UH-HUH.

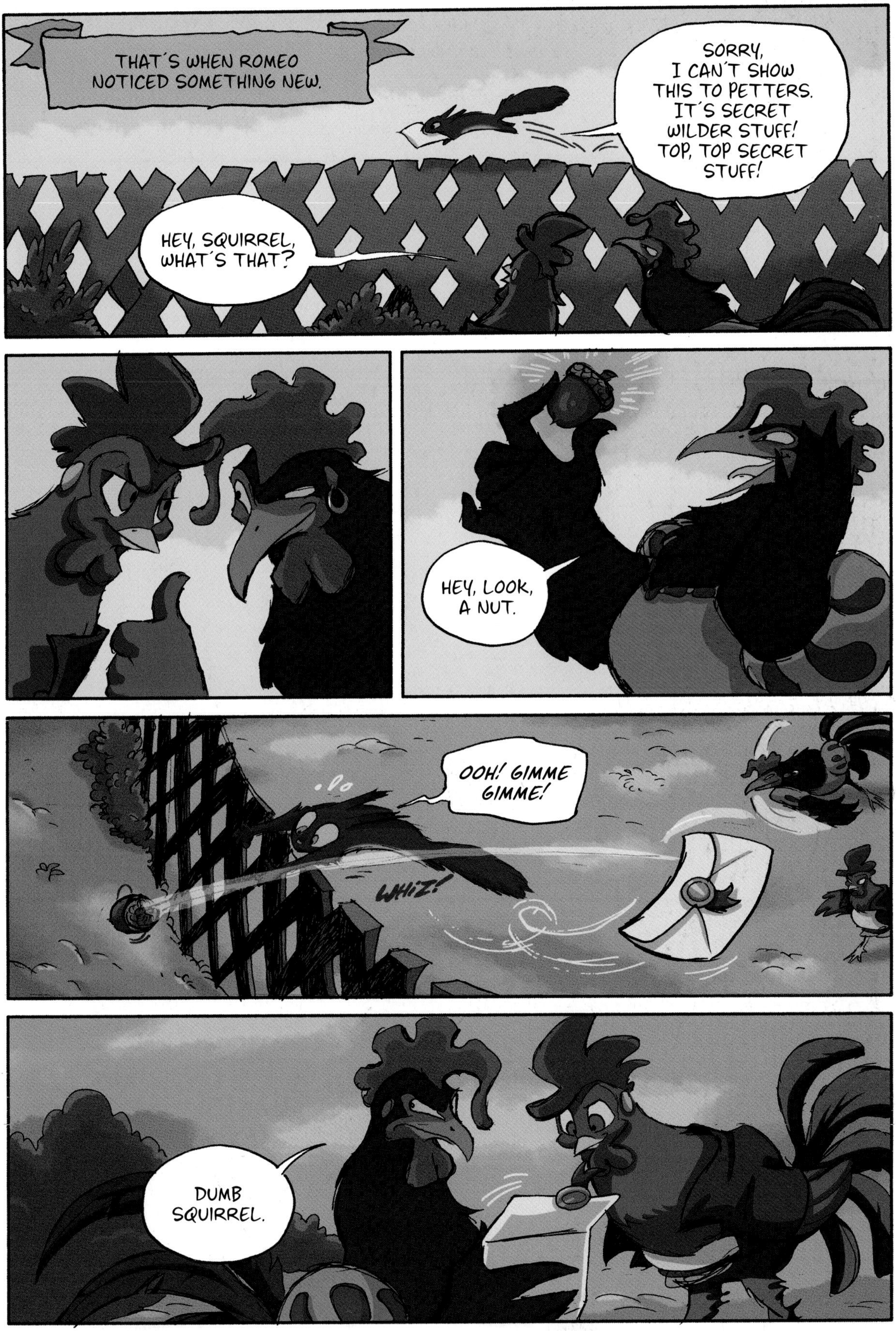

THAT´S WHEN ROMEO NOTICED SOMETHING NEW.
SORRY, I CAN´T SHOW THIS TO PETTERS. IT´S SECRET WILDER STUFF! TOP, TOP SECRET STUFF!
HEY, SQUIRREL, WHAT´S THAT?
HEY, LOOK, A NUT.
OOH! GIMME GIMME!
WHIZ!
DUMB SQUIRREL.

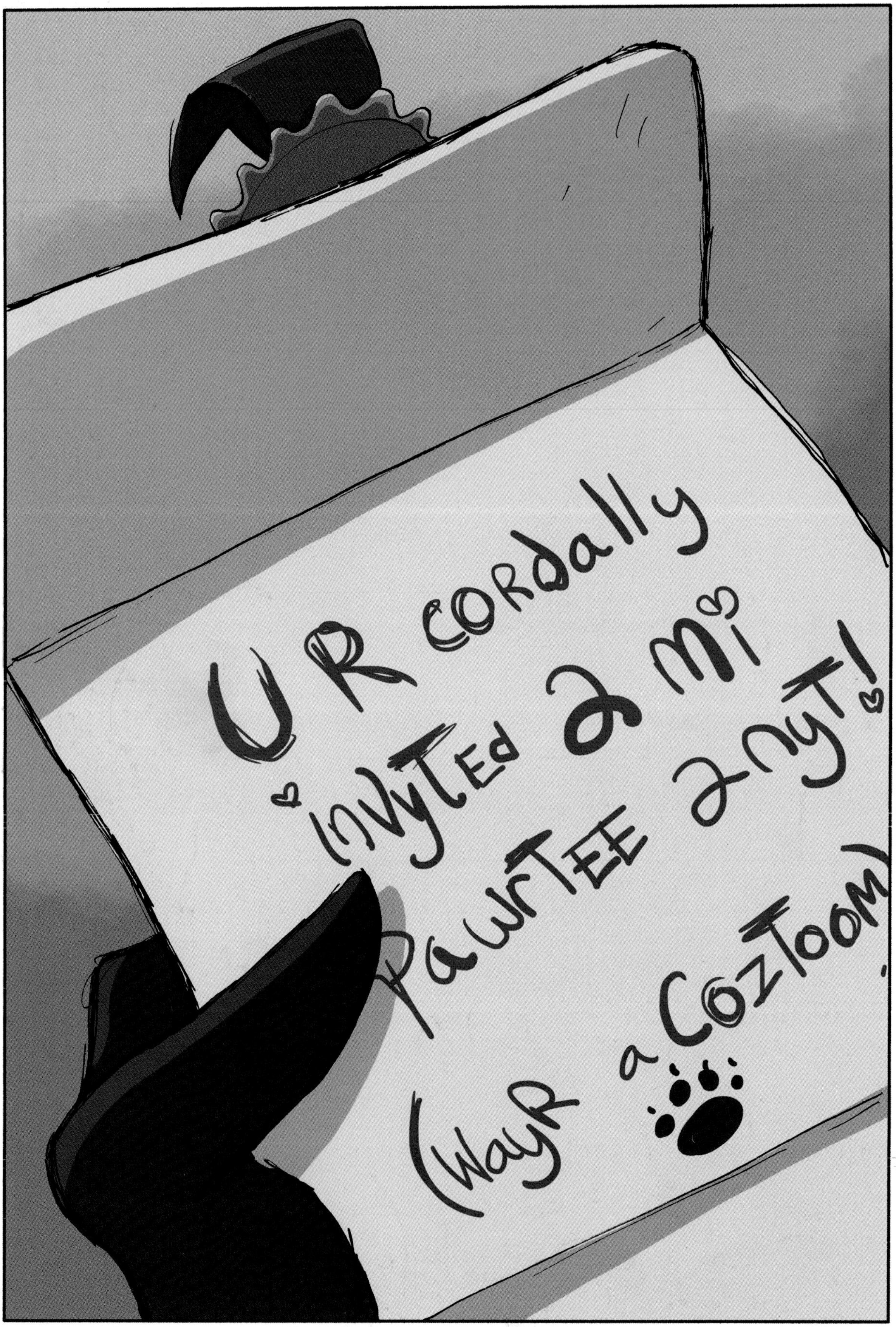
U R cordally
invyted 2 mi
PawrTEE 2nyT!
(WayR a CozToom)

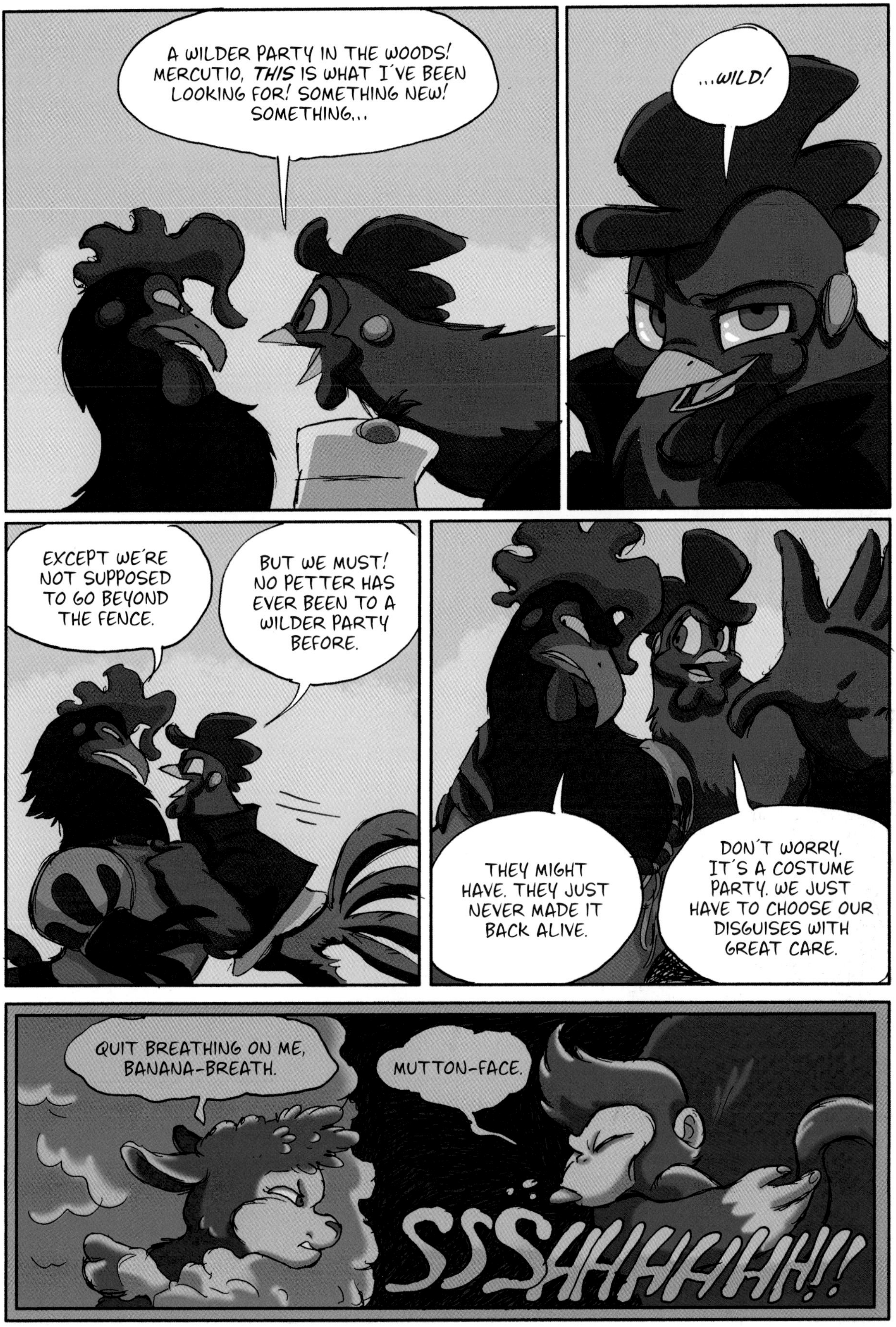
A WILDER PARTY IN THE WOODS! MERCUTIO, THIS IS WHAT I´VE BEEN LOOKING FOR! SOMETHING NEW! SOMETHING...
...WILD!
EXCEPT WE´RE NOT SUPPOSED TO GO BEYOND THE FENCE.
BUT WE MUST! NO PETTER HAS EVER BEEN TO A WILDER PARTY BEFORE.
THEY MIGHT HAVE. THEY JUST NEVER MADE IT BACK ALIVE.
DON´T WORRY. IT´S A COSTUME PARTY. WE JUST HAVE TO CHOOSE OUR DISGUISES WITH GREAT CARE.
QUIT BREATHING ON ME, BANANA-BREATH.
MUTTON-FACE.
SSSHHHHHH!!

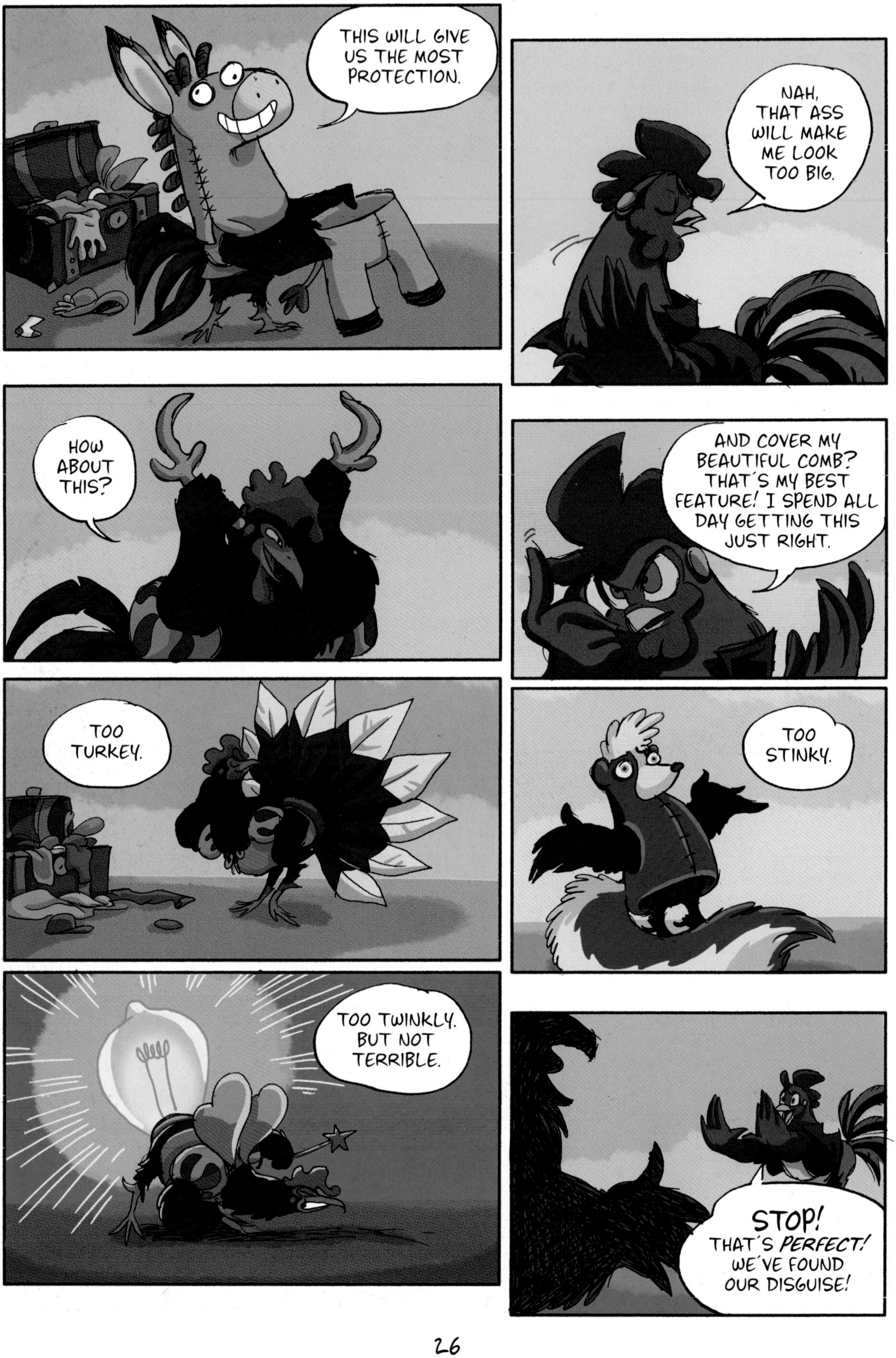
THIS WILL GIVE US THE MOST PROTECTION.
NAH, THAT ASS WILL MAKE ME LOOK TOO BIG.
HOW ABOUT THIS?
AND COVER MY BEAUTIFUL COMB? THAT´S MY BEST FEATURE! I SPEND ALL DAY GETTING THIS JUST RIGHT.
TOO TURKEY.
TOO STINKY.
TOO TWINKLY. BUT NOT TERRIBLE.
STOP! THAT´S *PERFECT!* WE´VE FOUND OUR DISGUISE!

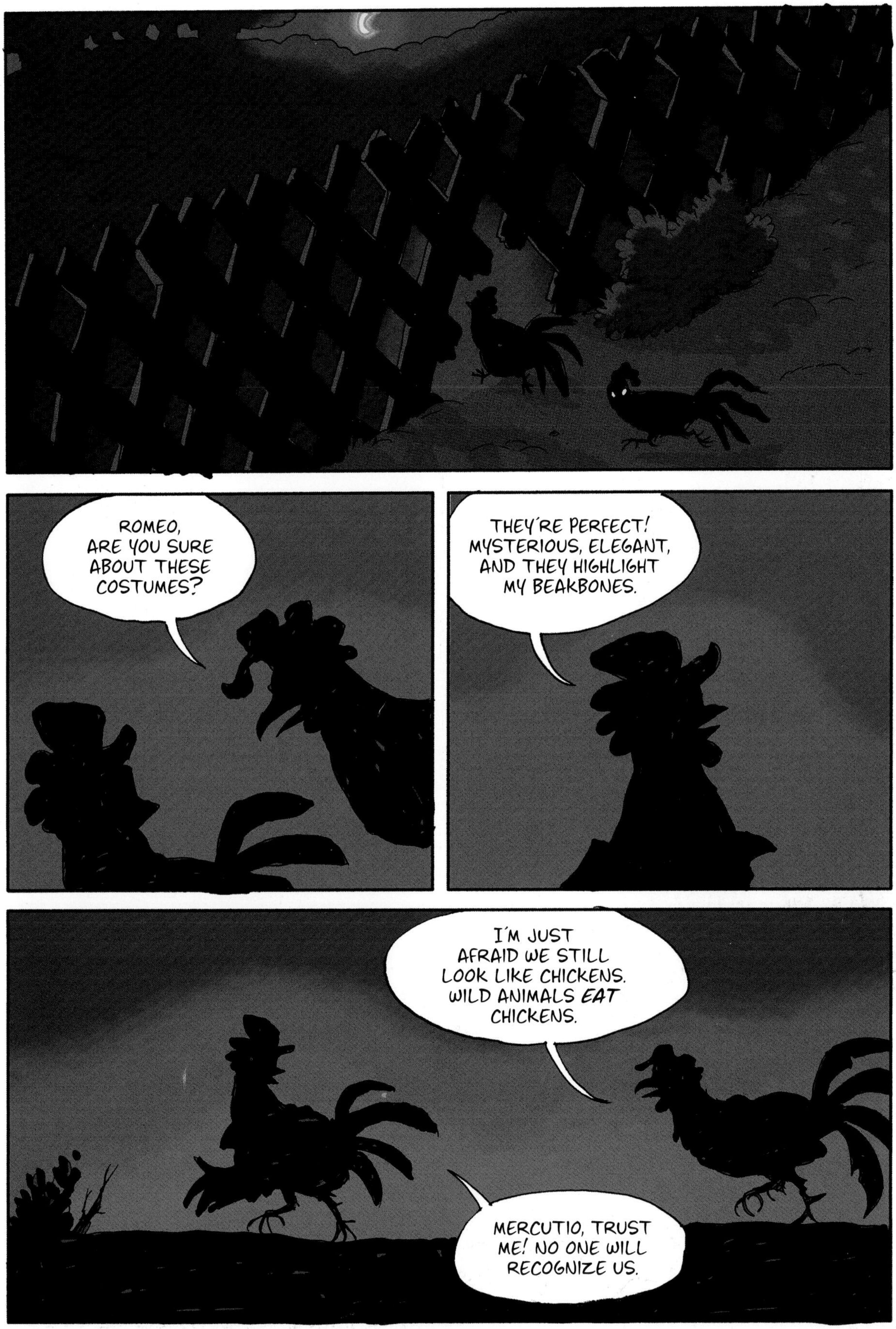
ROMEO, ARE YOU SURE ABOUT THESE COSTUMES?
THEY´RE PERFECT! MYSTERIOUS, ELEGANT, AND THEY HIGHLIGHT MY BEAKBONES.
I´M JUST AFRAID WE STILL LOOK LIKE CHICKENS. WILD ANIMALS *EAT* CHICKENS.
MERCUTIO, TRUST ME! NO ONE WILL RECOGNIZE US.

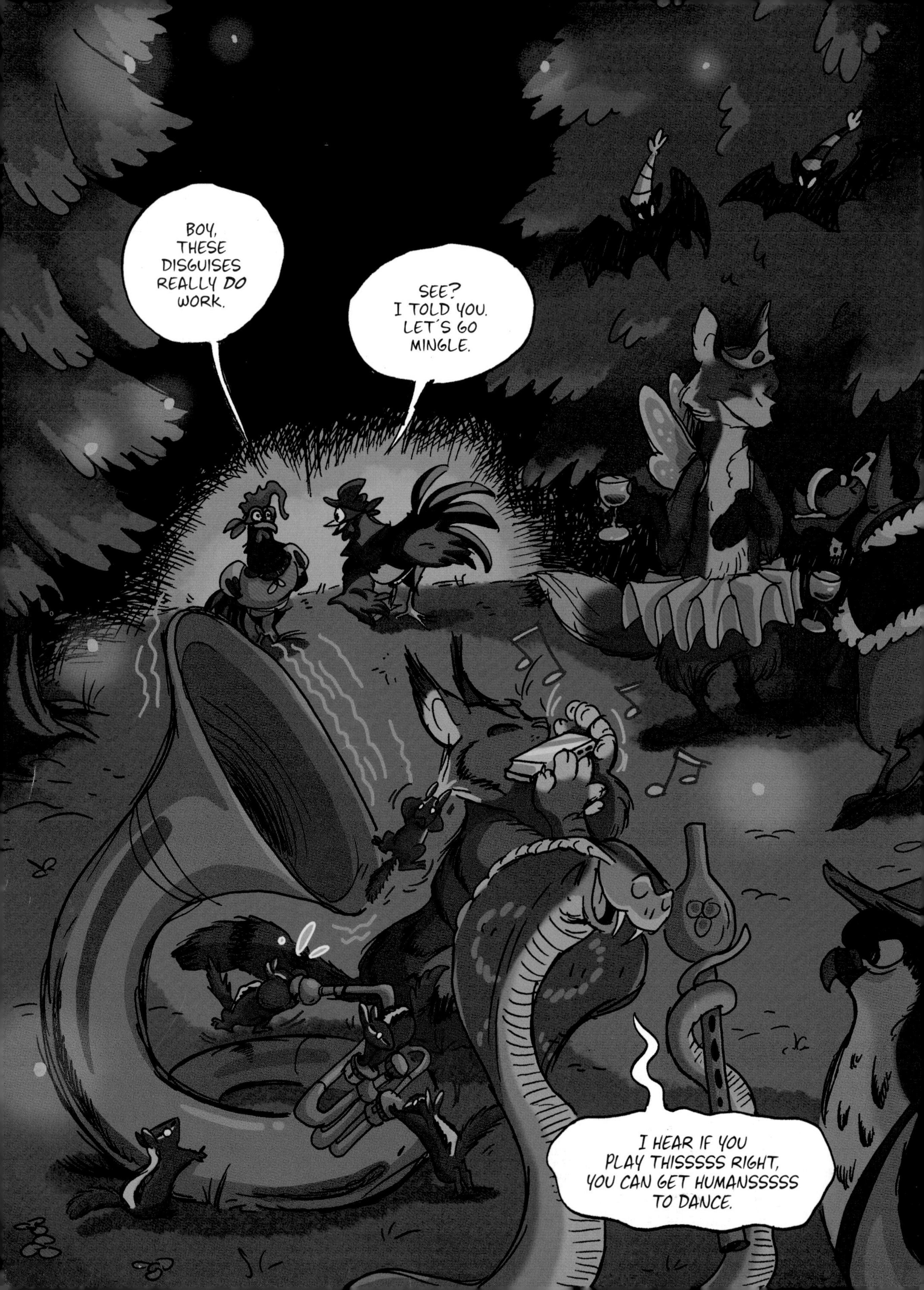
BOY, THESE DISGUISES REALLY *DO* WORK.
SEE? I TOLD YOU. LET'S GO MINGLE.
I HEAR IF YOU PLAY THISSSSS RIGHT, YOU CAN GET HUMANSSSSS TO DANCE.

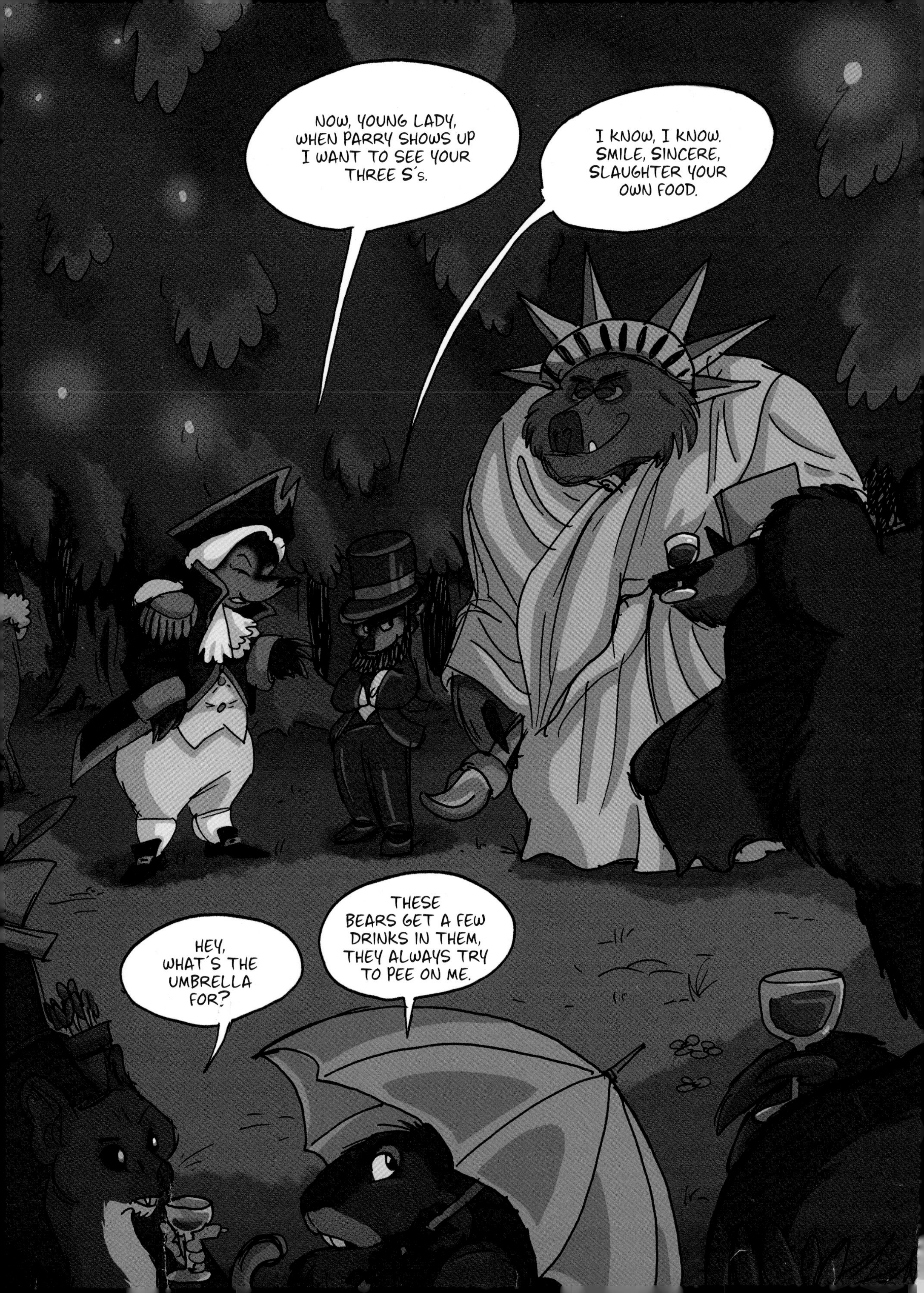
NOW, YOUNG LADY, WHEN PARRY SHOWS UP I WANT TO SEE YOUR THREE S´s.
I KNOW, I KNOW. SMILE, SINCERE, SLAUGHTER YOUR OWN FOOD.
HEY, WHAT´S THE UMBRELLA FOR?
THESE BEARS GET A FEW DRINKS IN THEM, THEY ALWAYS TRY TO PEE ON ME.

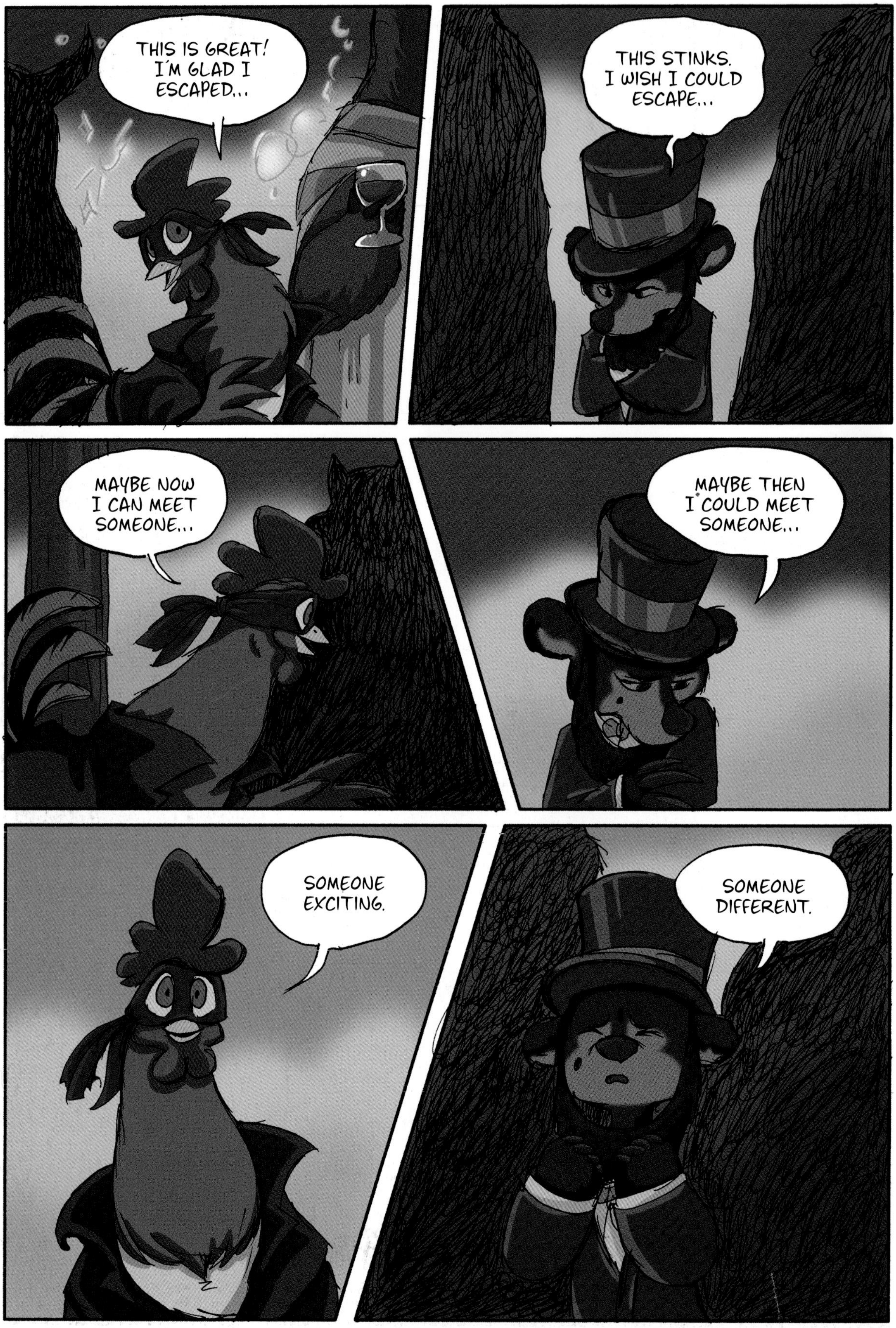
THIS IS GREAT! I'M GLAD I ESCAPED...
THIS STINKS. I WISH I COULD ESCAPE...
MAYBE NOW I CAN MEET SOMEONE...
MAYBE THEN I COULD MEET SOMEONE...
SOMEONE EXCITING.
SOMEONE DIFFERENT.

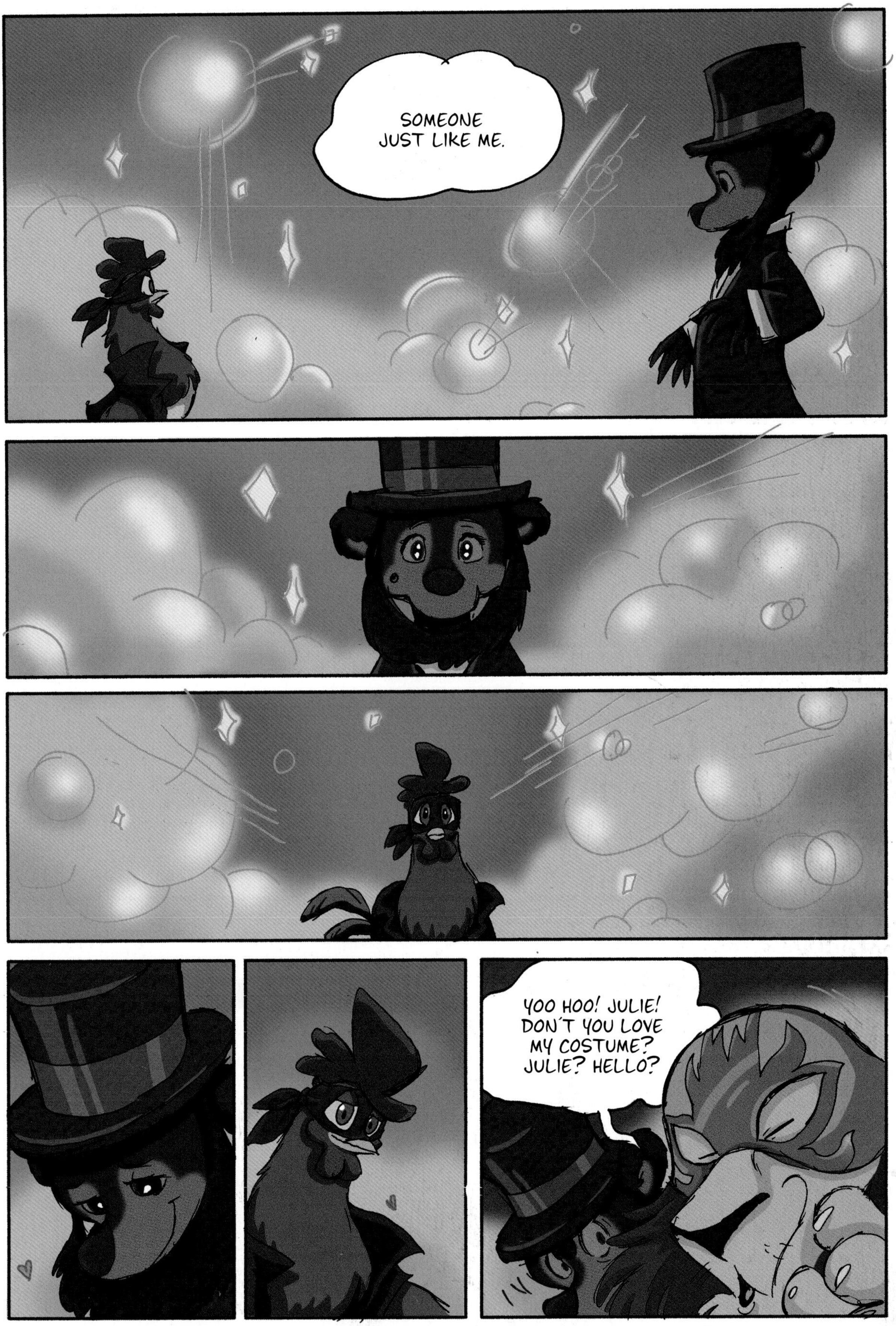
SOMEONE JUST LIKE ME.
YOO HOO! JULIE! DON'T YOU LOVE MY COSTUME? JULIE? HELLO?

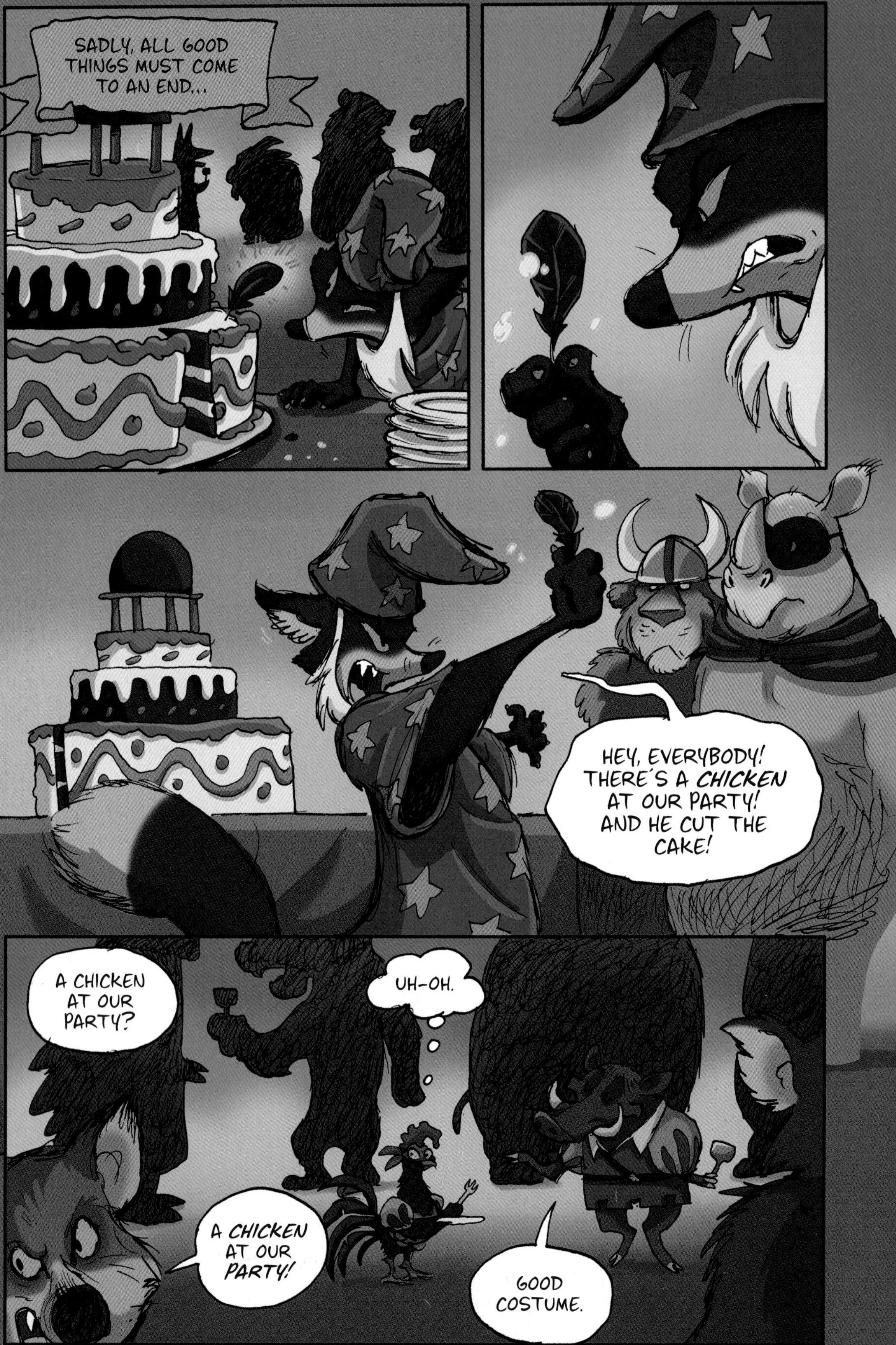
SADLY, ALL GOOD THINGS MUST COME TO AN END...
HEY, EVERYBODY! THERE'S A *CHICKEN* AT OUR PARTY! AND HE CUT THE CAKE!
A CHICKEN AT OUR PARTY?
UH-OH.
A *CHICKEN* AT OUR *PARTY!*
GOOD COSTUME.

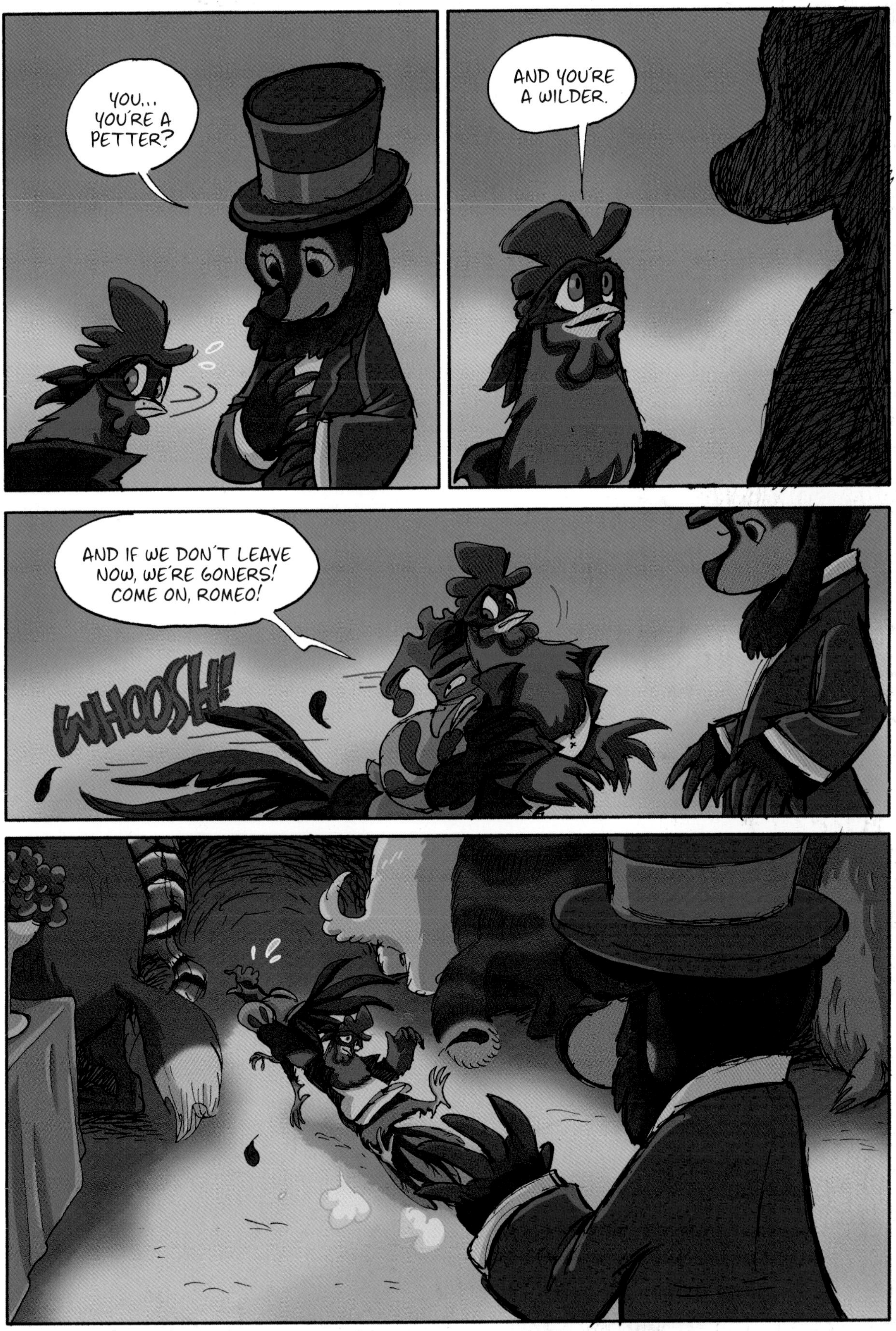
YOU... YOU'RE A PETTER?
AND YOU'RE A WILDER.
AND IF WE DON'T LEAVE NOW, WE'RE GONERS! COME ON, ROMEO!
WHOOSH!

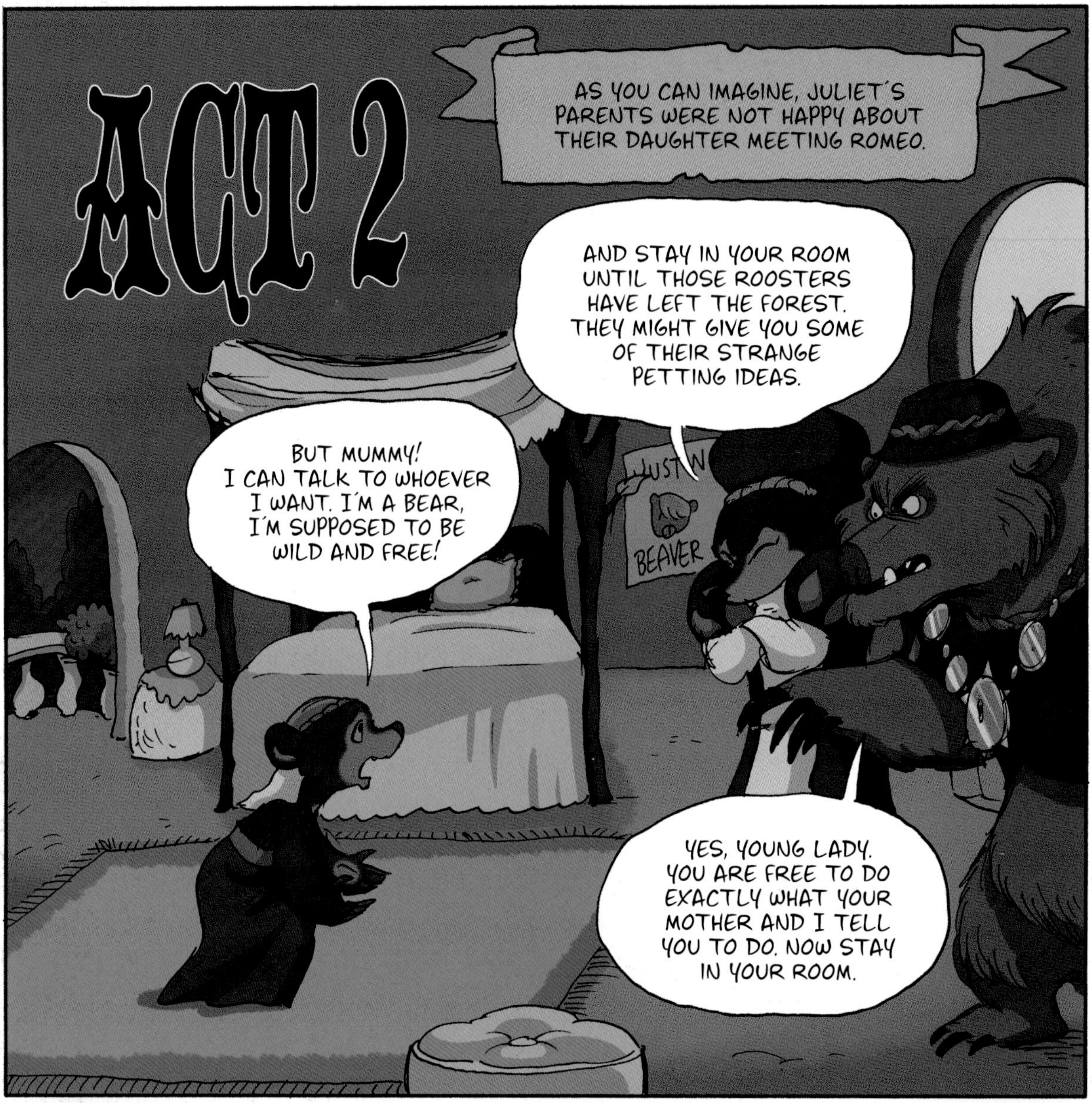
ACT 2
AS YOU CAN IMAGINE, JULIET´S PARENTS WERE NOT HAPPY ABOUT THEIR DAUGHTER MEETING ROMEO.
AND STAY IN YOUR ROOM UNTIL THOSE ROOSTERS HAVE LEFT THE FOREST. THEY MIGHT GIVE YOU SOME OF THEIR STRANGE PETTING IDEAS.
BUT MUMMY! I CAN TALK TO WHOEVER I WANT. I´M A BEAR, I´M SUPPOSED TO BE WILD AND FREE!
JUST W
BEAVER
YES, YOUNG LADY. YOU ARE FREE TO DO EXACTLY WHAT YOUR MOTHER AND I TELL YOU TO DO. NOW STAY IN YOUR ROOM.

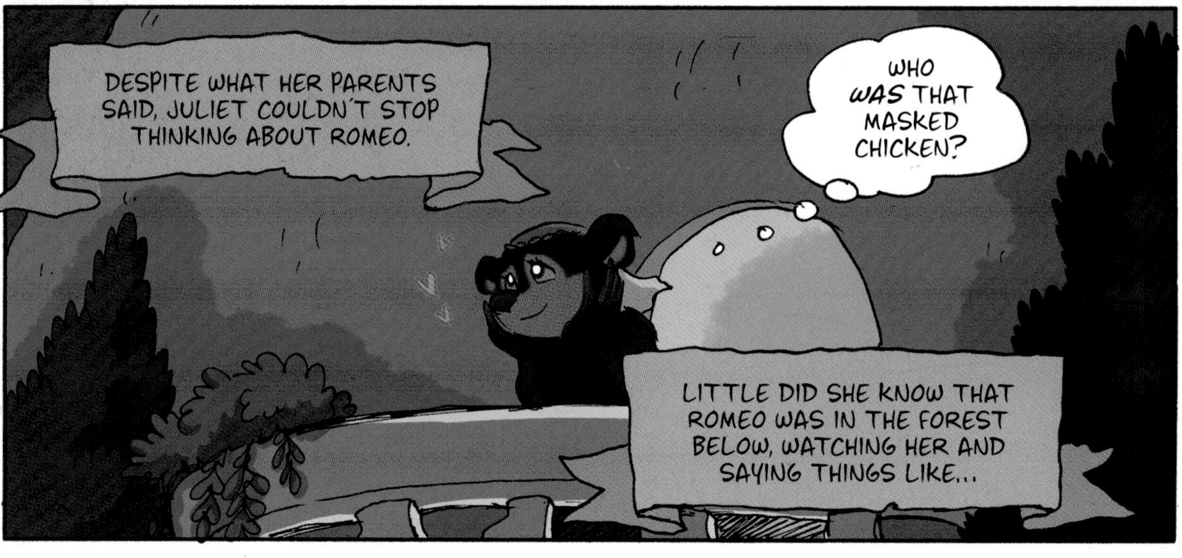
DESPITE WHAT HER PARENTS SAID, JULIET COULDN´T STOP THINKING ABOUT ROMEO.
WHO *WAS* THAT MASKED CHICKEN?
LITTLE DID SHE KNOW THAT ROMEO WAS IN THE FOREST BELOW, WATCHING HER AND SAYING THINGS LIKE...

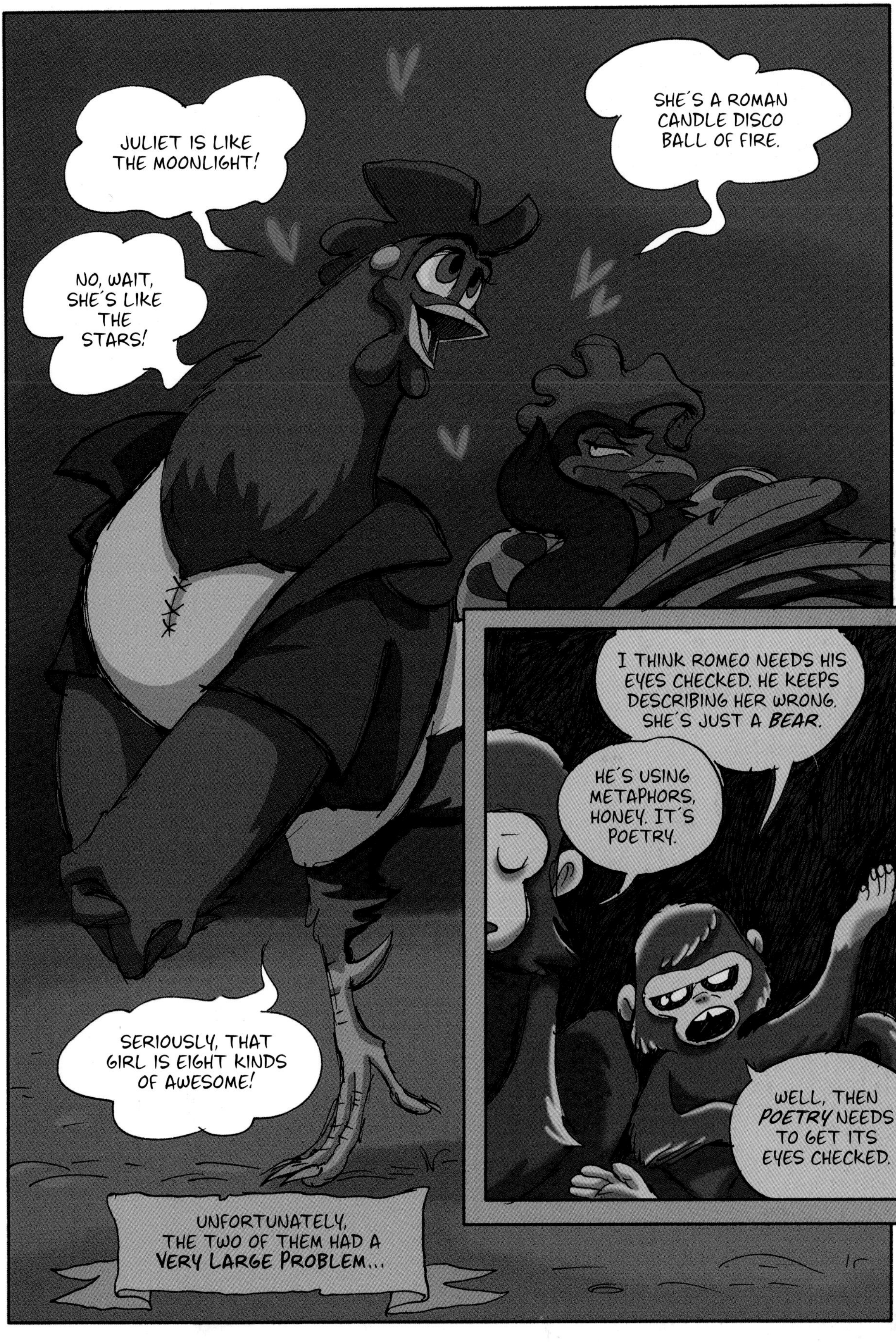
JULIET IS LIKE THE MOONLIGHT!
SHE'S A ROMAN CANDLE DISCO BALL OF FIRE.
NO, WAIT, SHE'S LIKE THE STARS!
I THINK ROMEO NEEDS HIS EYES CHECKED. HE KEEPS DESCRIBING HER WRONG. SHE'S JUST A *BEAR*.
HE'S USING METAPHORS, HONEY. IT'S POETRY.
SERIOUSLY, THAT GIRL IS EIGHT KINDS OF AWESOME!
WELL, THEN *POETRY* NEEDS TO GET ITS EYES CHECKED.
UNFORTUNATELY, THE TWO OF THEM HAD A VERY LARGE PROBLEM...

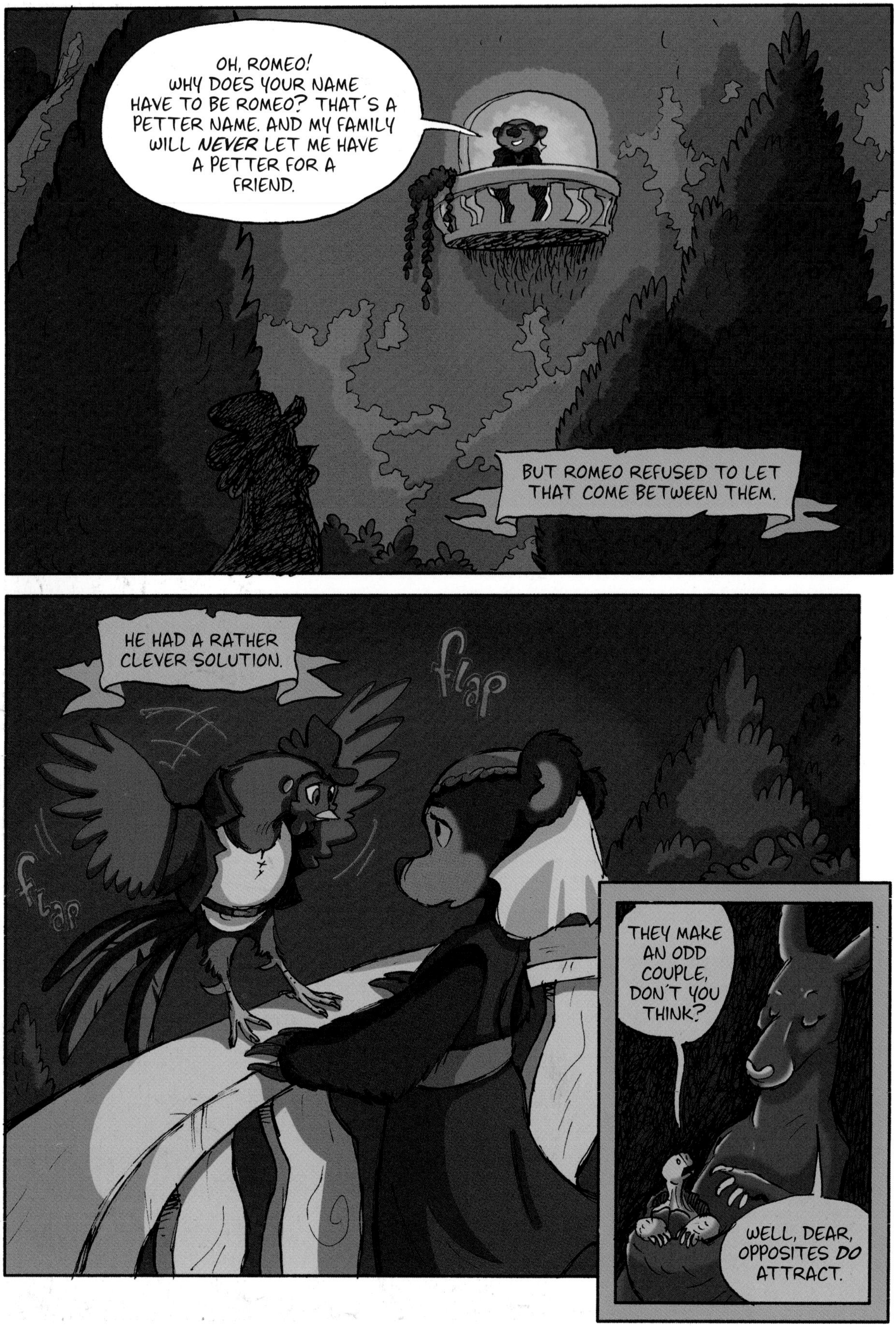
OH, ROMEO! WHY DOES YOUR NAME HAVE TO BE ROMEO? THAT'S A PETTER NAME. AND MY FAMILY WILL NEVER LET ME HAVE A PETTER FOR A FRIEND.
BUT ROMEO REFUSED TO LET THAT COME BETWEEN THEM.
HE HAD A RATHER CLEVER SOLUTION.
flap
flap
THEY MAKE AN ODD COUPLE, DON'T YOU THINK?
WELL, DEAR, OPPOSITES DO ATTRACT.

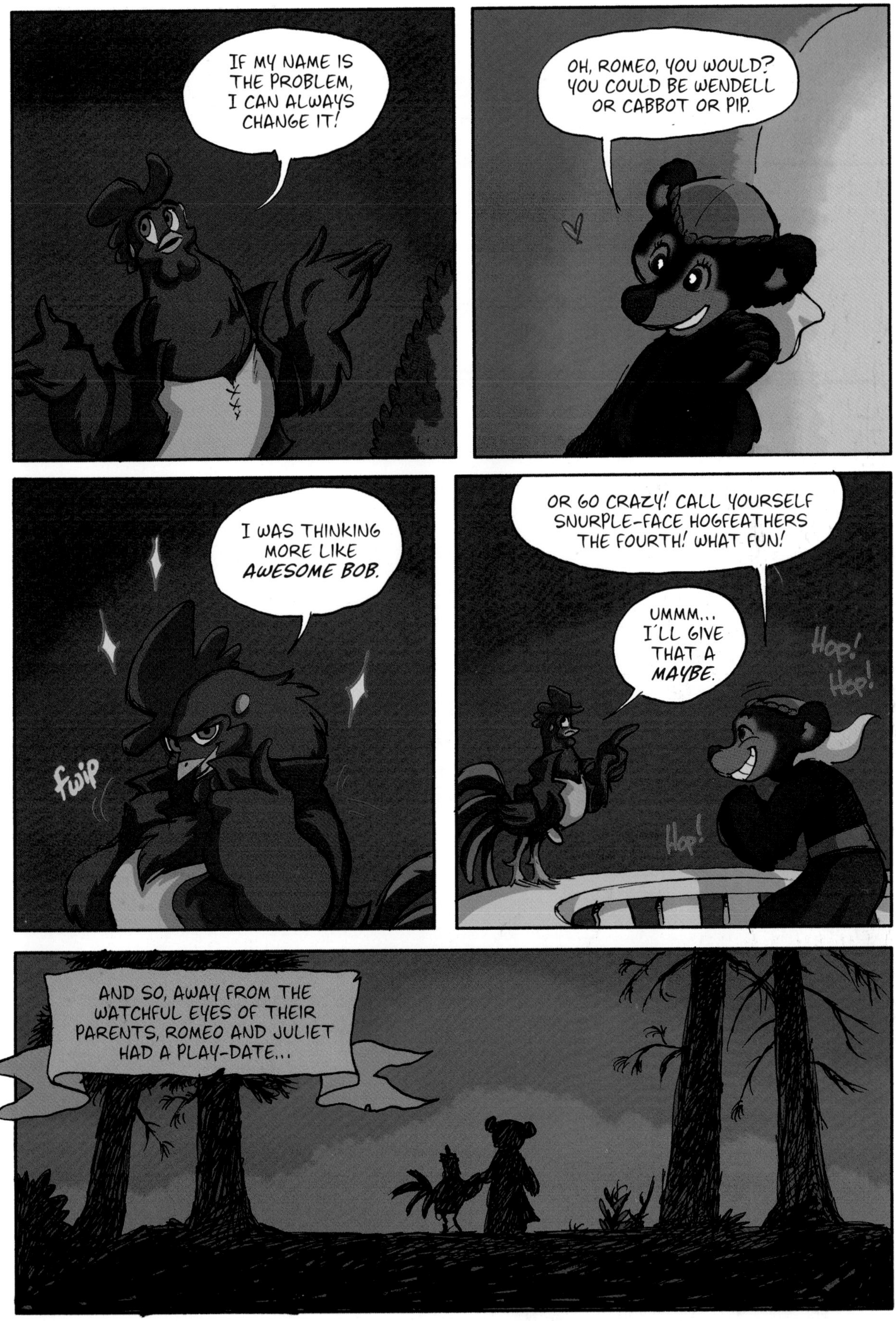

IF MY NAME IS THE PROBLEM, I CAN ALWAYS CHANGE IT!
OH, ROMEO, YOU WOULD? YOU COULD BE WENDELL OR CABBOT OR PIP.
I WAS THINKING MORE LIKE AWESOME BOB.
fwip
OR GO CRAZY! CALL YOURSELF SNURPLE-FACE HOGFEATHERS THE FOURTH! WHAT FUN!
UMMM... I'LL GIVE THAT A MAYBE.
Hop! Hop!
Hop!
AND SO, AWAY FROM THE WATCHFUL EYES OF THEIR PARENTS, ROMEO AND JULIET HAD A PLAY-DATE...

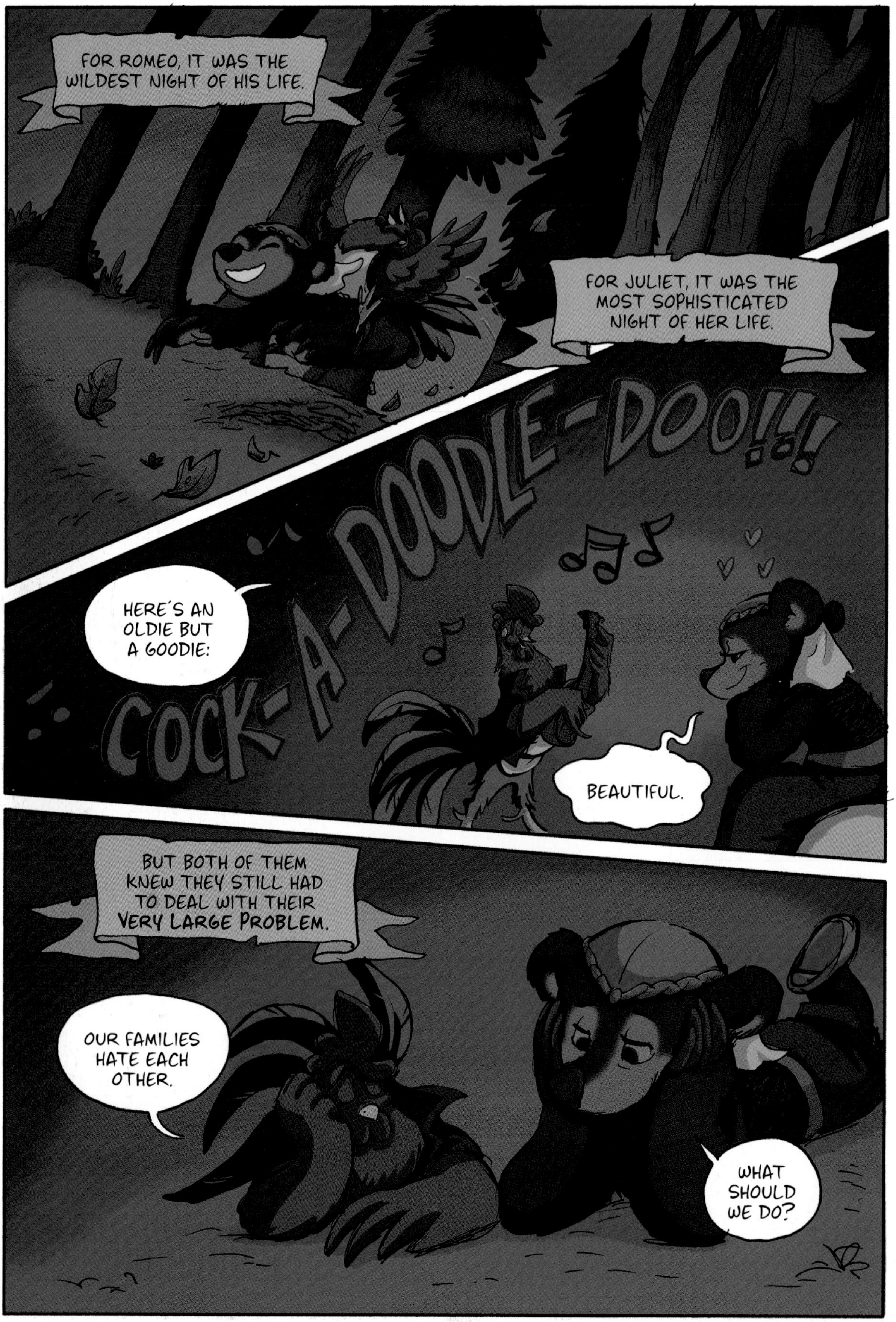

FOR ROMEO, IT WAS THE WILDEST NIGHT OF HIS LIFE.
FOR JULIET, IT WAS THE MOST SOPHISTICATED NIGHT OF HER LIFE.
HERE'S AN OLDIE BUT A GOODIE:
COCK-A-DOODLE-DOO!!!
BEAUTIFUL.
BUT BOTH OF THEM KNEW THEY STILL HAD TO DEAL WITH THEIR VERY LARGE PROBLEM.
OUR FAMILIES HATE EACH OTHER.
WHAT SHOULD WE DO?

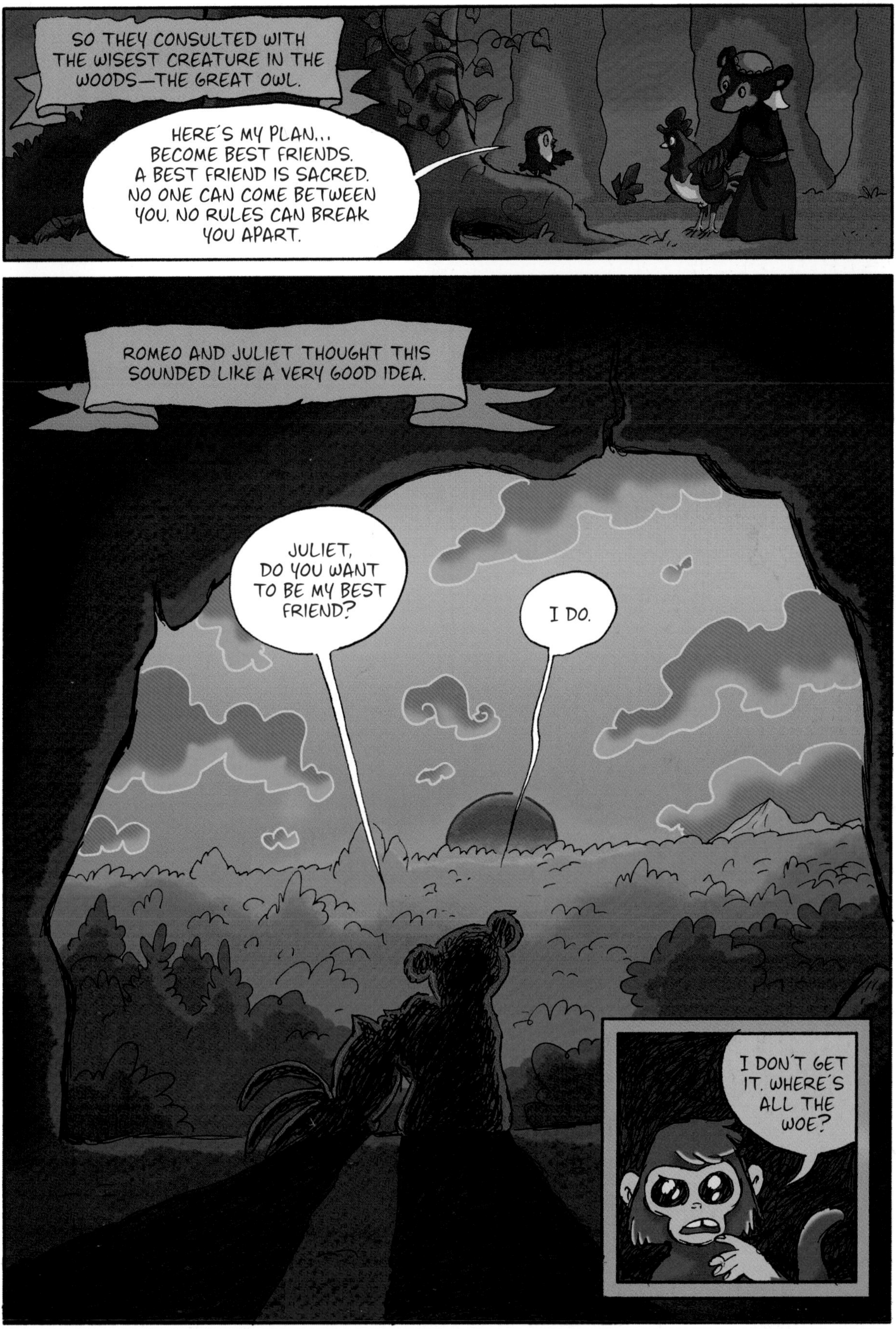
SO THEY CONSULTED WITH THE WISEST CREATURE IN THE WOODS—THE GREAT OWL.
HERE'S MY PLAN... BECOME BEST FRIENDS. A BEST FRIEND IS SACRED. NO ONE CAN COME BETWEEN YOU. NO RULES CAN BREAK YOU APART.
ROMEO AND JULIET THOUGHT THIS SOUNDED LIKE A VERY GOOD IDEA.
JULIET, DO YOU WANT TO BE MY BEST FRIEND?
I DO.
I DON'T GET IT. WHERE'S ALL THE WOE?

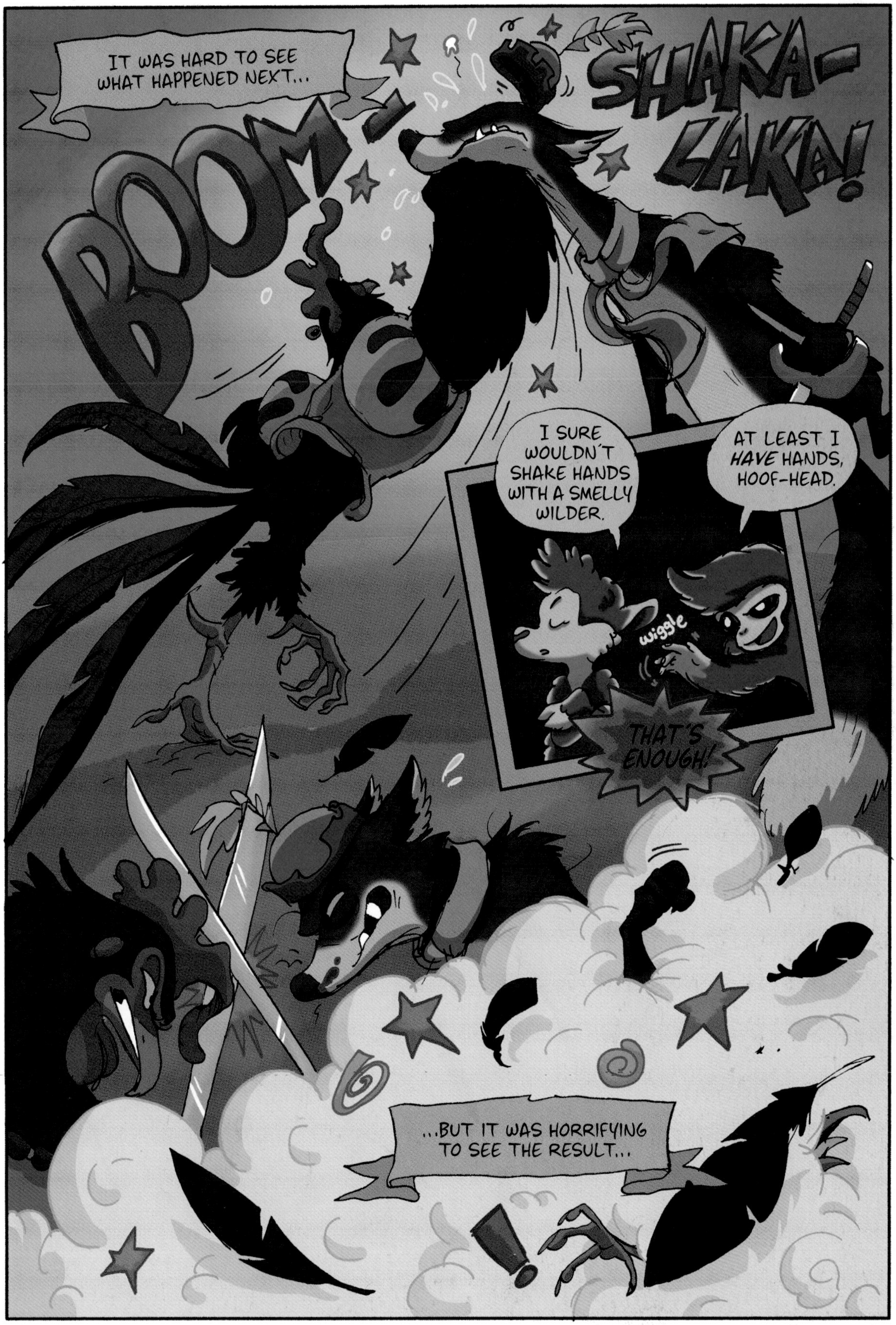
IT WAS HARD TO SEE WHAT HAPPENED NEXT...
BOOM!
SHAKA-LAKA!
I SURE WOULDN'T SHAKE HANDS WITH A SMELLY WILDER.
AT LEAST I HAVE HANDS, HOOF-HEAD.
wiggle
THAT'S ENOUGH!
...BUT IT WAS HORRIFYING TO SEE THE RESULT...

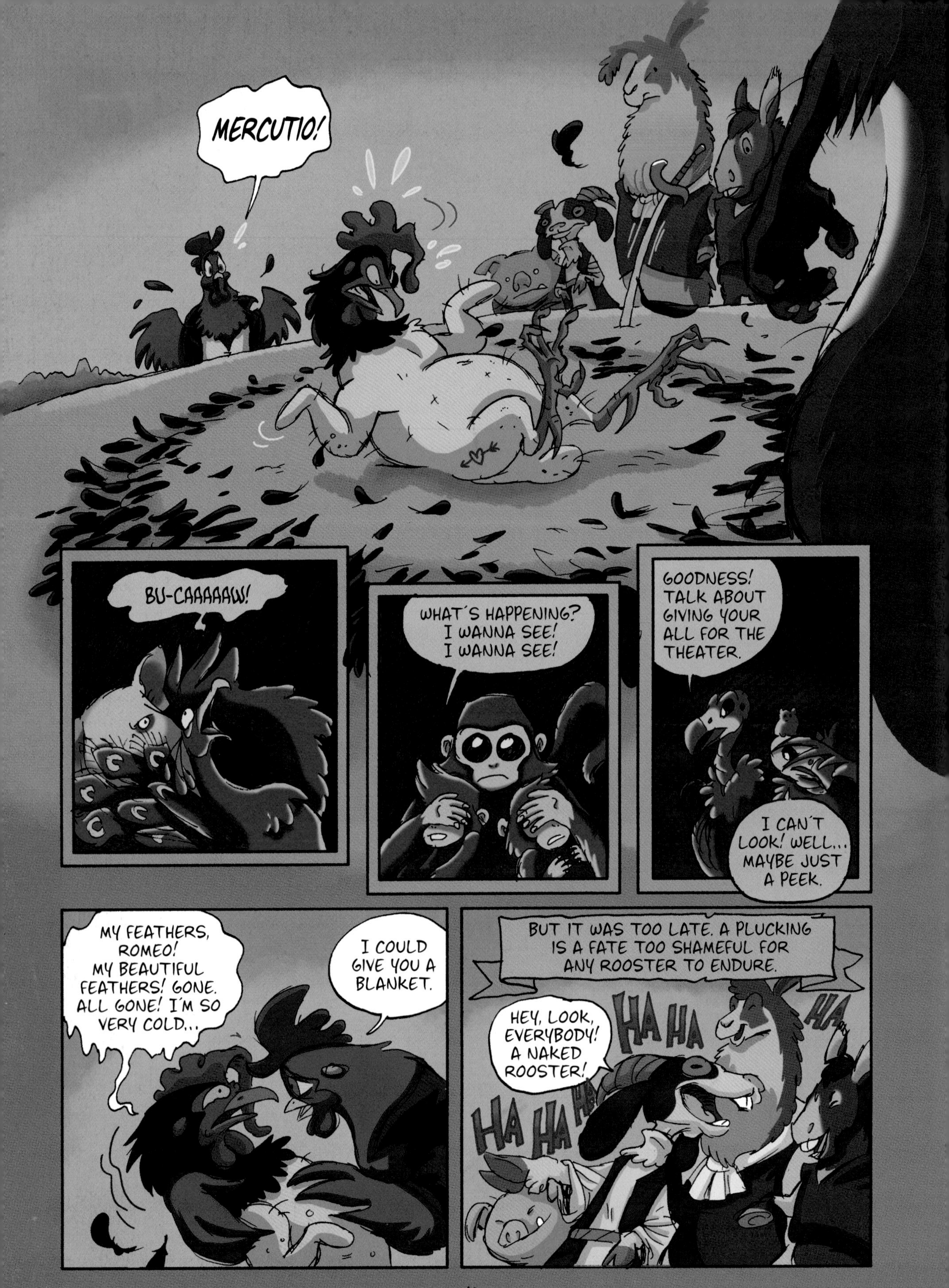
MERCUTIO!
BU-CAAAAAAW!
WHAT'S HAPPENING? I WANNA SEE! I WANNA SEE!
GOODNESS! TALK ABOUT GIVING YOUR ALL FOR THE THEATER.
I CAN'T LOOK! WELL... MAYBE JUST A PEEK.
MY FEATHERS, ROMEO! MY BEAUTIFUL FEATHERS! GONE. ALL GONE! I'M SO VERY COLD...
I COULD GIVE YOU A BLANKET.
BUT IT WAS TOO LATE. A PLUCKING IS A FATE TOO SHAMEFUL FOR ANY ROOSTER TO ENDURE.
HEY, LOOK, EVERYBODY! A NAKED ROOSTER!
HA HA
HA
HA HA HA

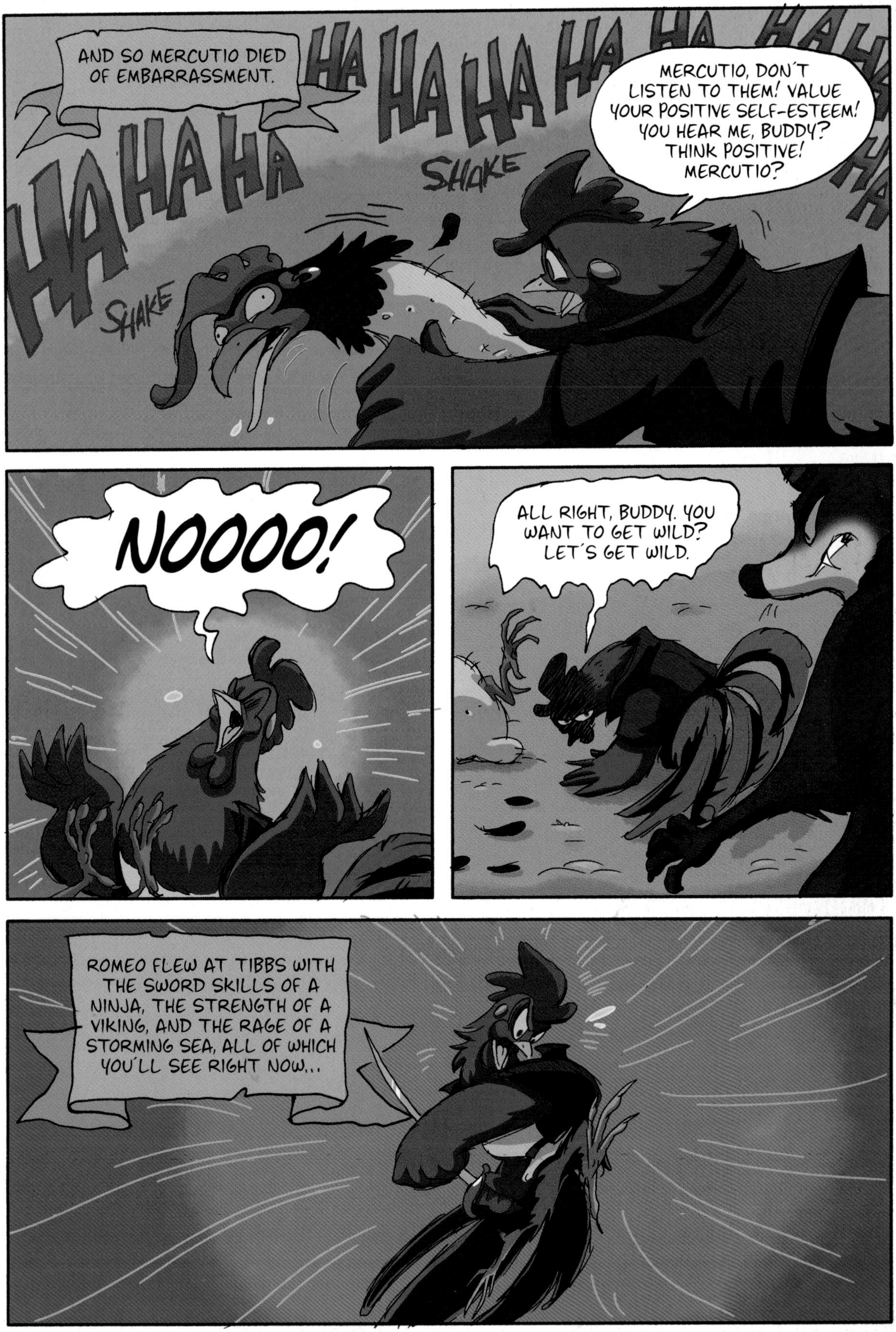
AND SO MERCUTIO DIED OF EMBARRASSMENT.
HAHAHA HA HA HA HA HA HA HA HA HA HA
SHAKE
SHAKE
MERCUTIO, DON´T LISTEN TO THEM! VALUE YOUR POSITIVE SELF-ESTEEM! YOU HEAR ME, BUDDY? THINK POSITIVE! MERCUTIO?
NOOOO!
ALL RIGHT, BUDDY. YOU WANT TO GET WILD? LET´S GET WILD.
ROMEO FLEW AT TIBBS WITH THE SWORD SKILLS OF A NINJA, THE STRENGTH OF A VIKING, AND THE RAGE OF A STORMING SEA, ALL OF WHICH YOU´LL SEE RIGHT NOW...

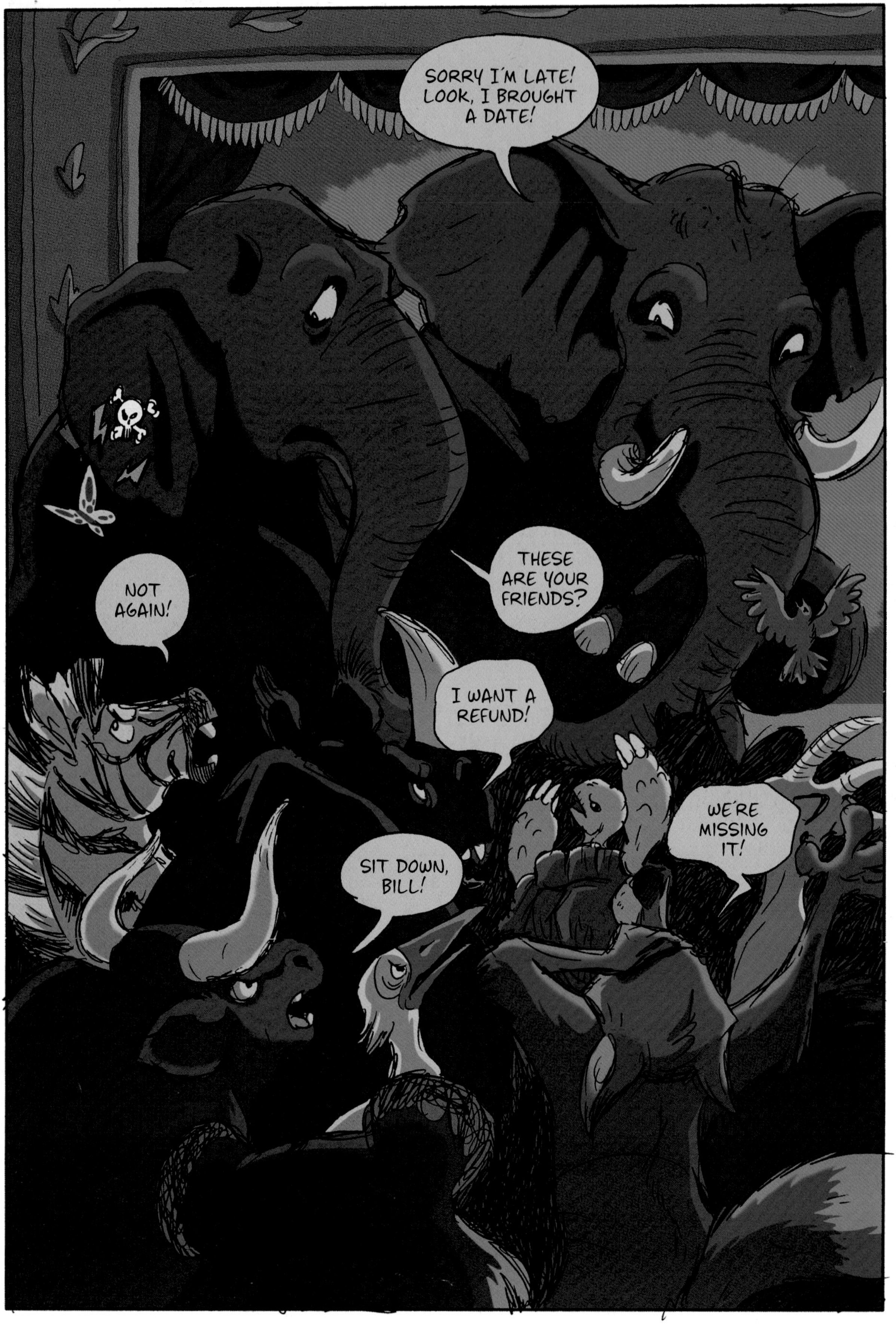
SORRY I'M LATE! LOOK, I BROUGHT A DATE!
NOT AGAIN!
THESE ARE YOUR FRIENDS?
I WANT A REFUND!
SIT DOWN, BILL!
WE'RE MISSING IT!

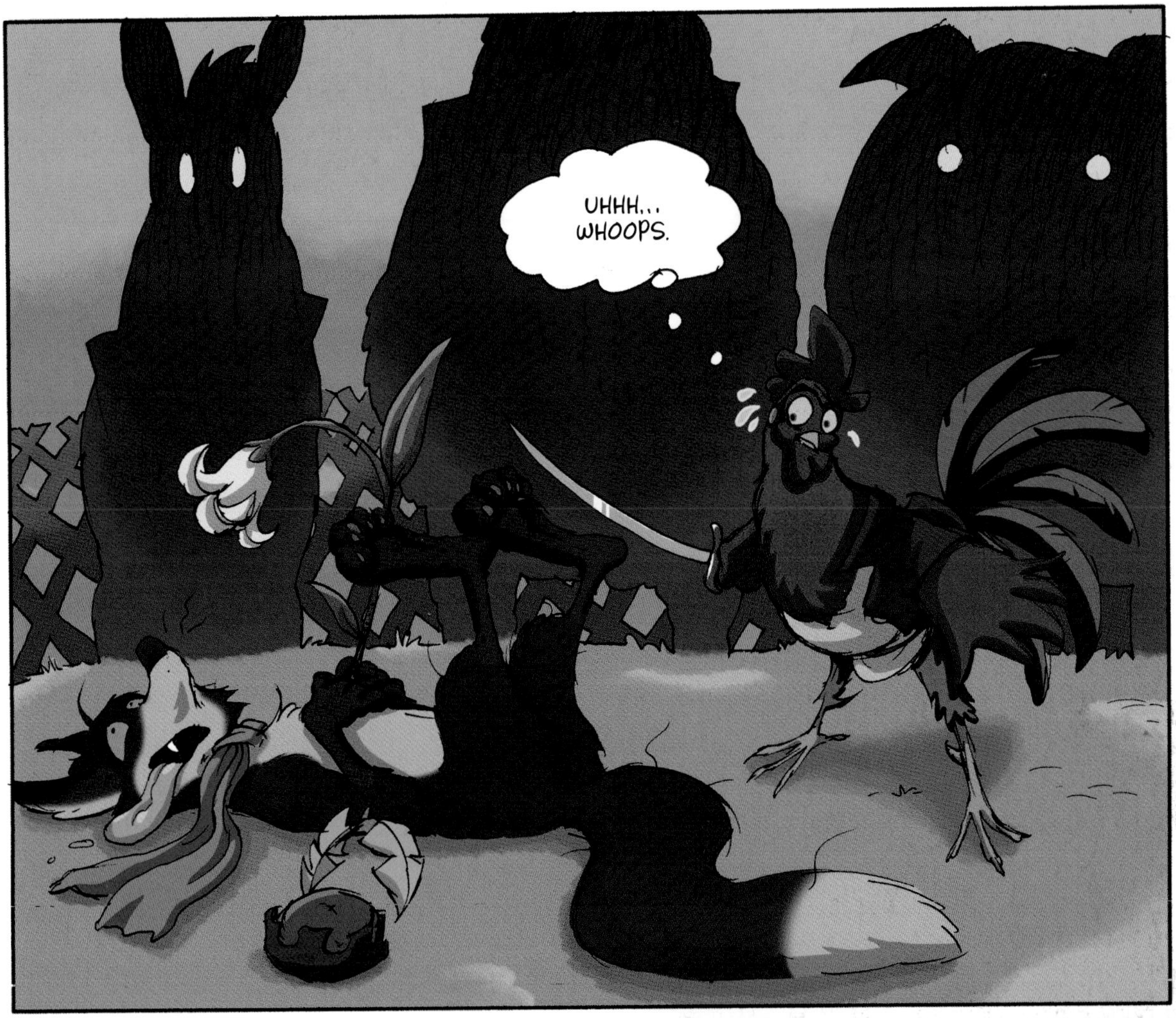
UHHH...
WHOOPS.

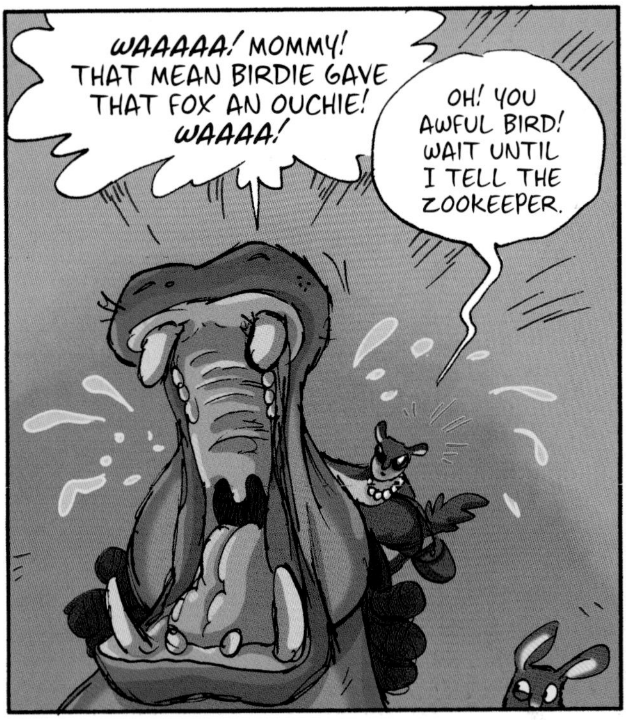
WAAAAA! MOMMY! THAT MEAN BIRDIE GAVE THAT FOX AN OUCHIE! WAAAA!
OH! YOU AWFUL BIRD! WAIT UNTIL I TELL THE ZOOKEEPER.

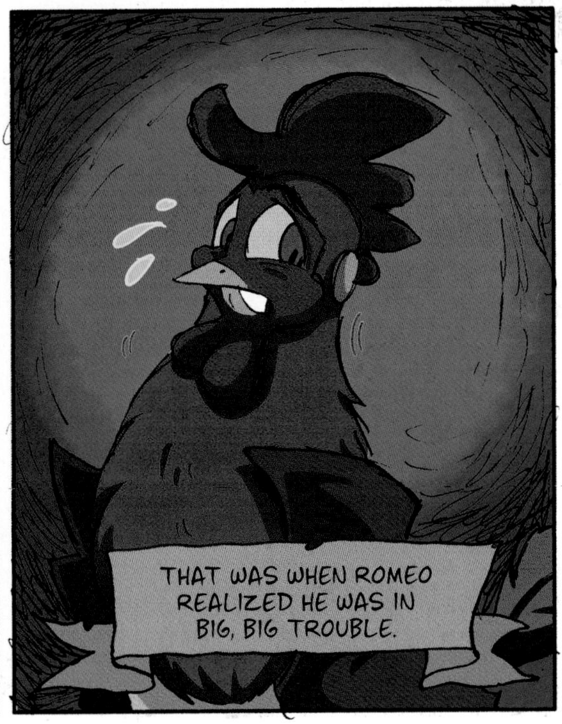
THAT WAS WHEN ROMEO REALIZED HE WAS IN BIG, BIG TROUBLE.

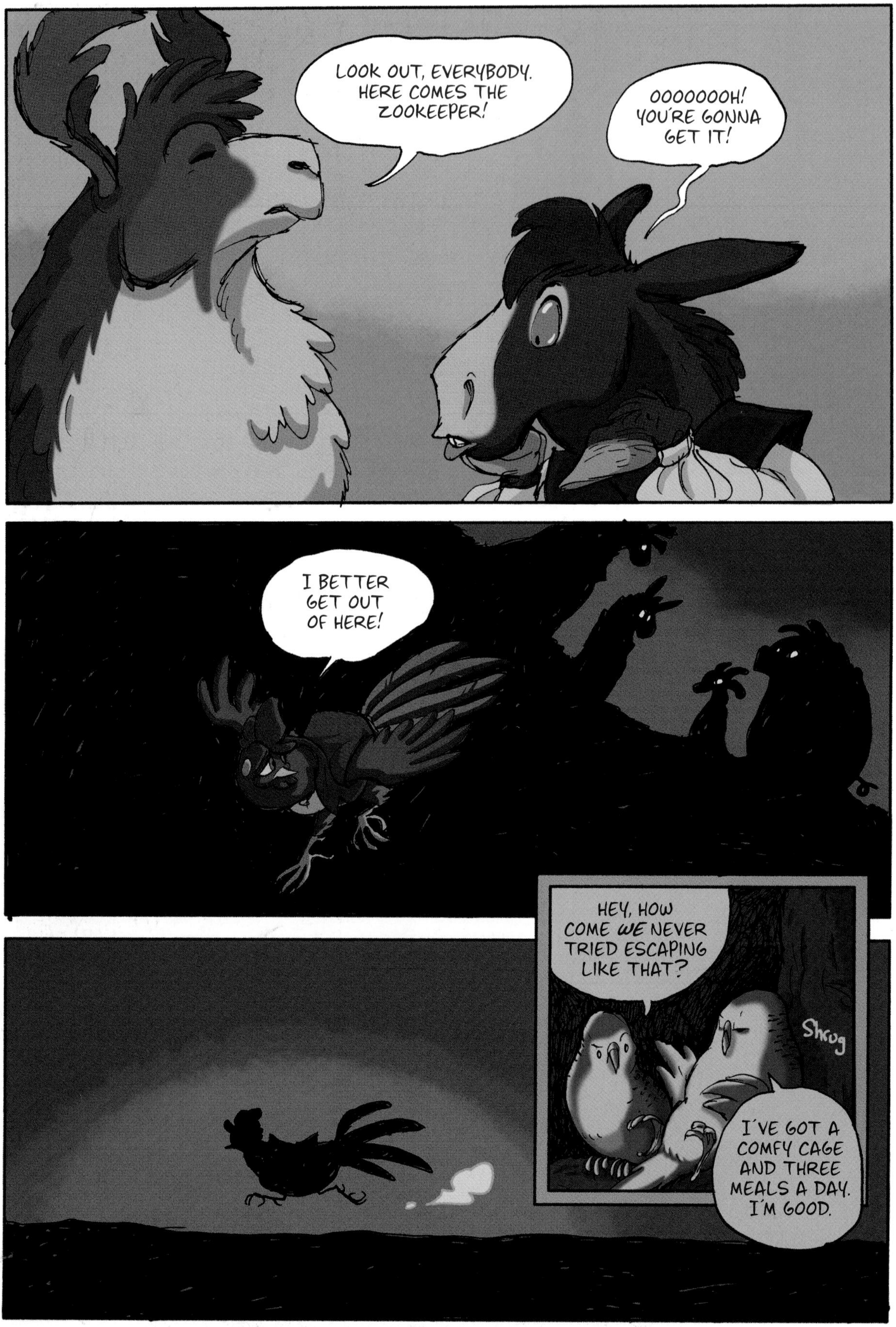
LOOK OUT, EVERYBODY. HERE COMES THE ZOOKEEPER!
OOOOOOOH! YOU'RE GONNA GET IT!
I BETTER GET OUT OF HERE!
HEY, HOW COME *WE* NEVER TRIED ESCAPING LIKE THAT?
Shrug
I'VE GOT A COMFY CAGE AND THREE MEALS A DAY. I'M GOOD.

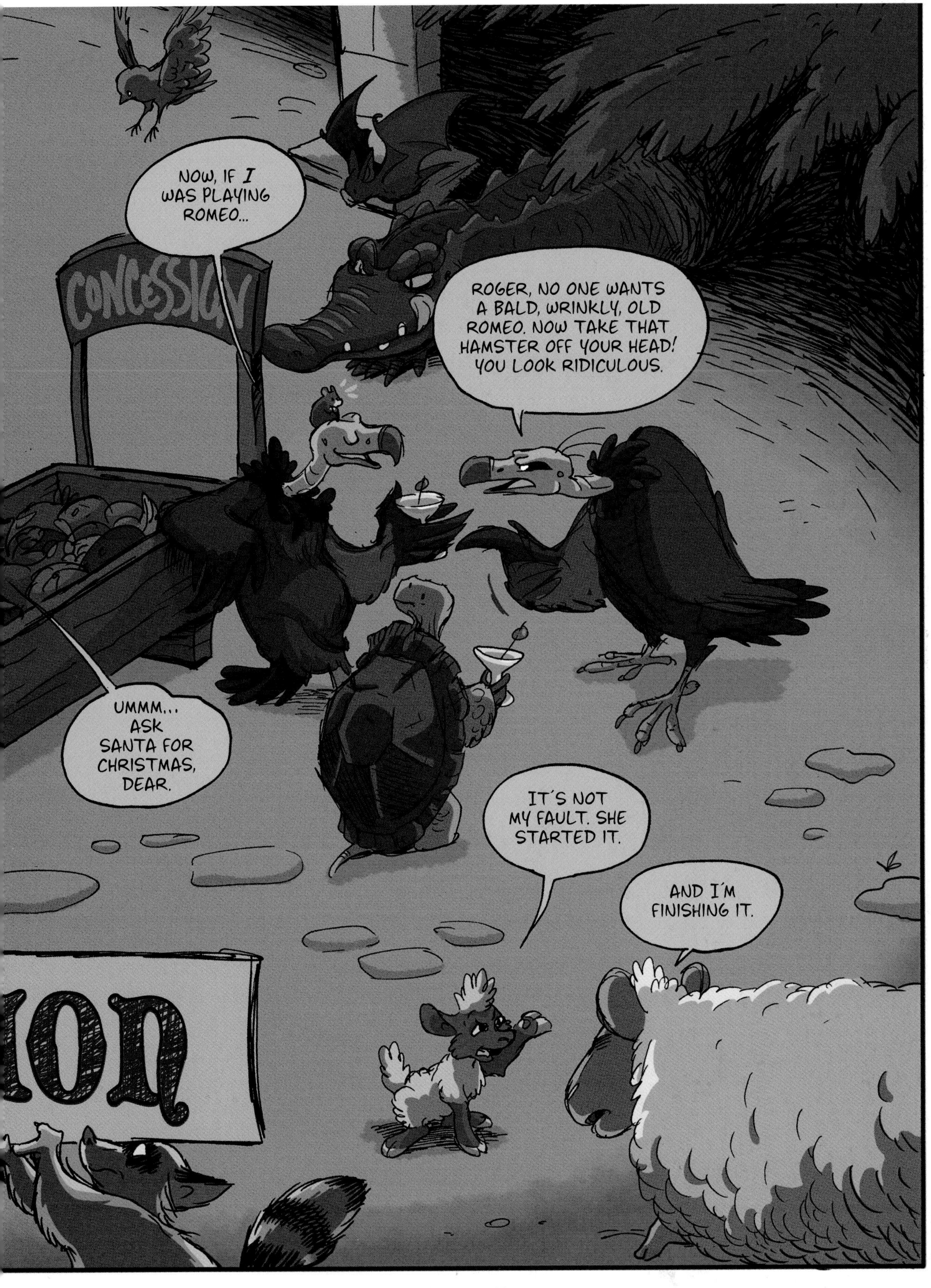
NOW, IF I WAS PLAYING ROMEO...
CONCESSION
ROGER, NO ONE WANTS A BALD, WRINKLY, OLD ROMEO. NOW TAKE THAT HAMSTER OFF YOUR HEAD! YOU LOOK RIDICULOUS.
UMMM... ASK SANTA FOR CHRISTMAS, DEAR.
IT'S NOT MY FAULT. SHE STARTED IT.
AND I'M FINISHING IT.
ION

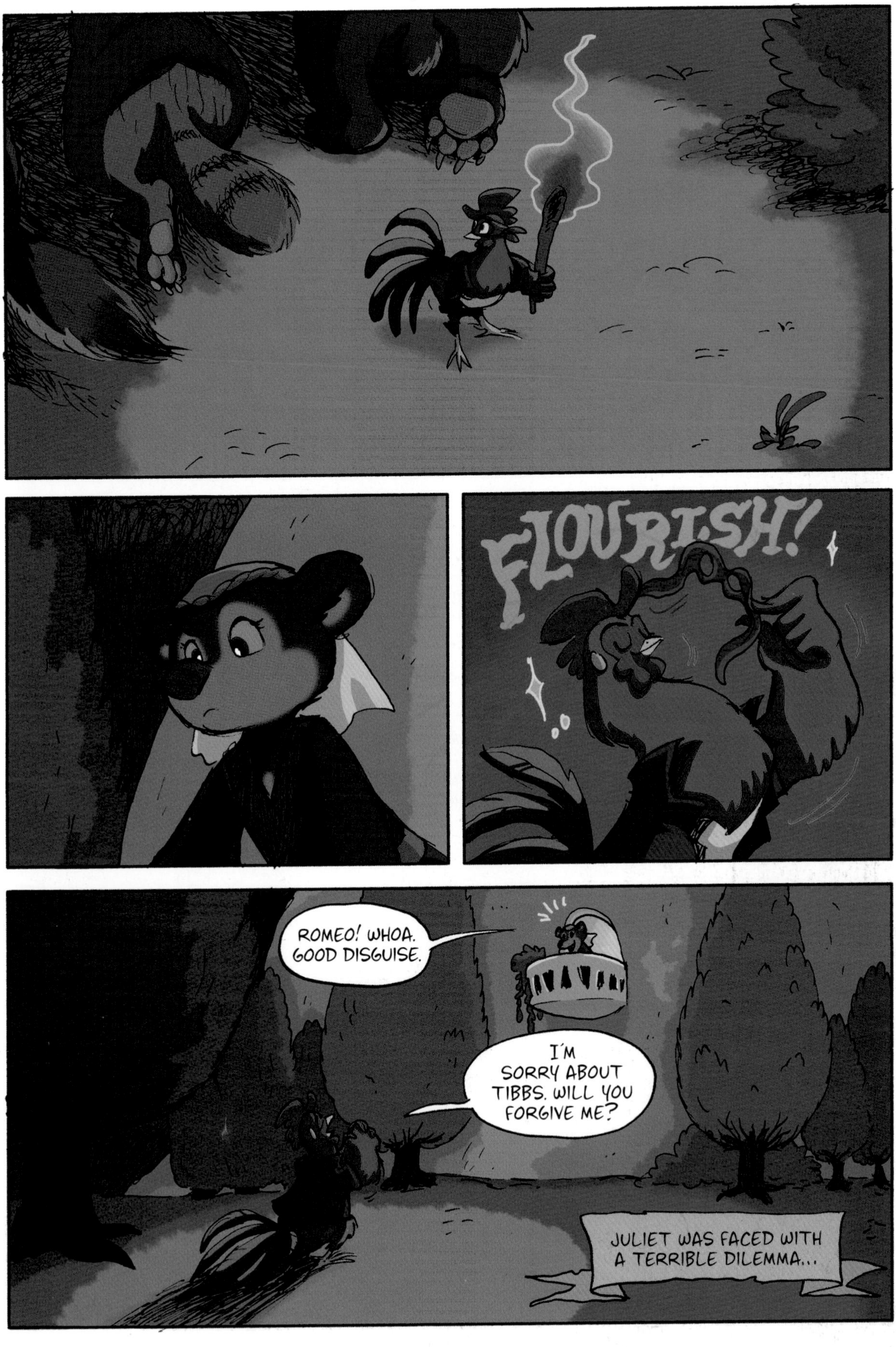
FLOURISH!
ROMEO! WHOA. GOOD DISGUISE.
I'M SORRY ABOUT TIBBS. WILL YOU FORGIVE ME?
JULIET WAS FACED WITH A TERRIBLE DILEMMA...

65

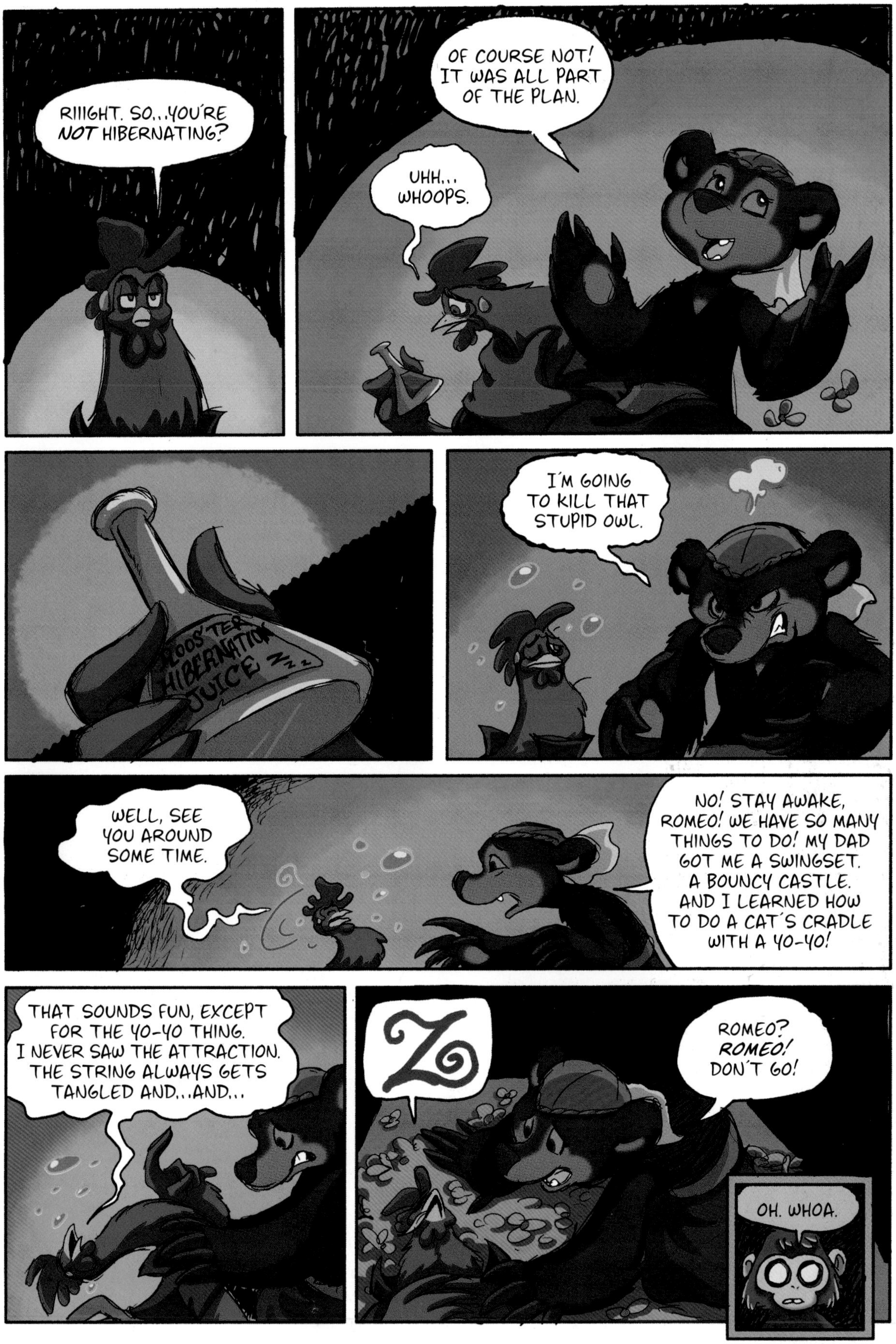
RIIIGHT. SO...YOU'RE NOT HIBERNATING?
OF COURSE NOT! IT WAS ALL PART OF THE PLAN.
UHH... WHOOPS.
ROOSTER HIBERNATION JUICE
I'M GOING TO KILL THAT STUPID OWL.
WELL, SEE YOU AROUND SOME TIME.
NO! STAY AWAKE, ROMEO! WE HAVE SO MANY THINGS TO DO! MY DAD GOT ME A SWINGSET. A BOUNCY CASTLE. AND I LEARNED HOW TO DO A CAT'S CRADLE WITH A YO-YO!
THAT SOUNDS FUN, EXCEPT FOR THE YO-YO THING. I NEVER SAW THE ATTRACTION. THE STRING ALWAYS GETS TANGLED AND...AND...
Z
ROMEO? ROMEO! DON'T GO!
OH. WHOA.

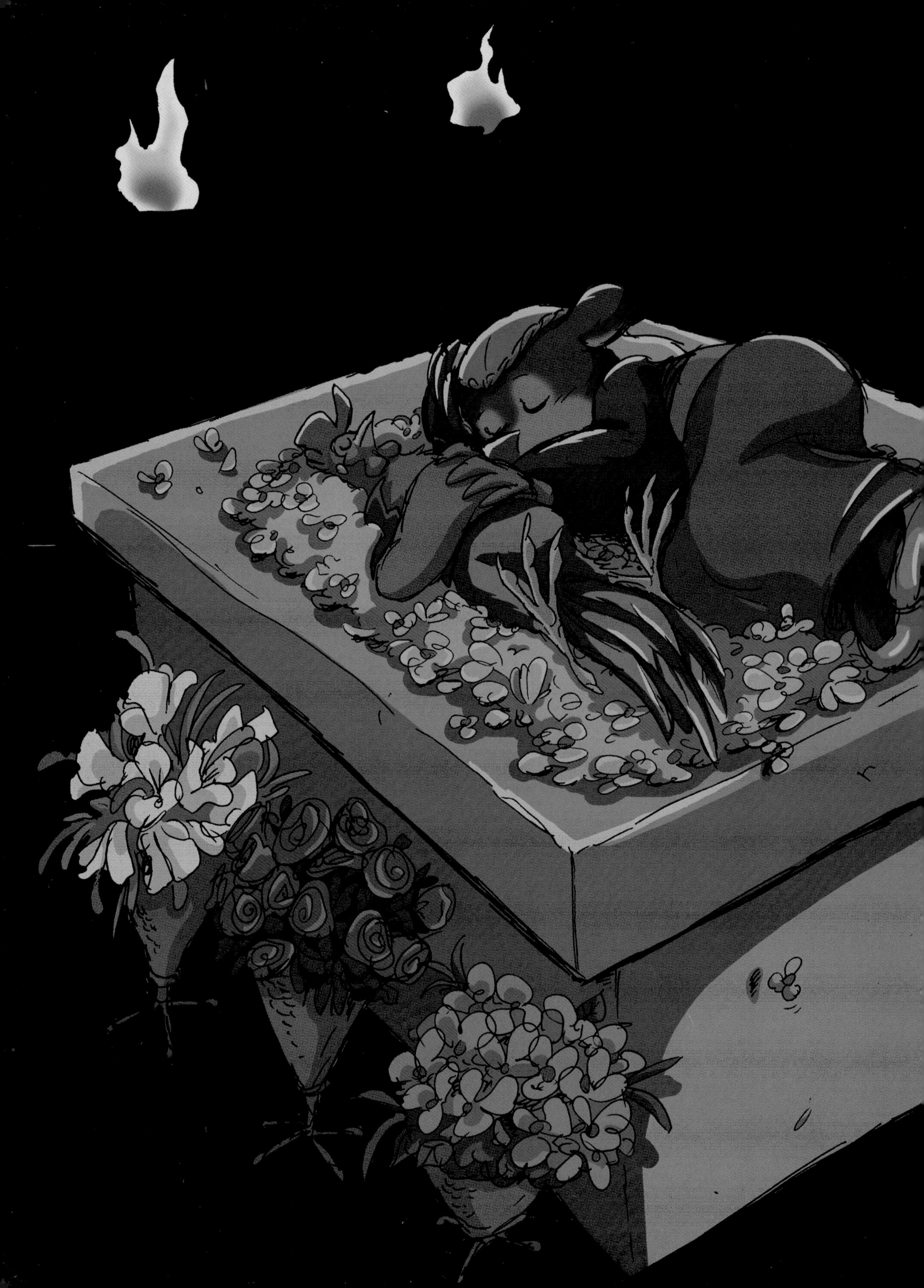

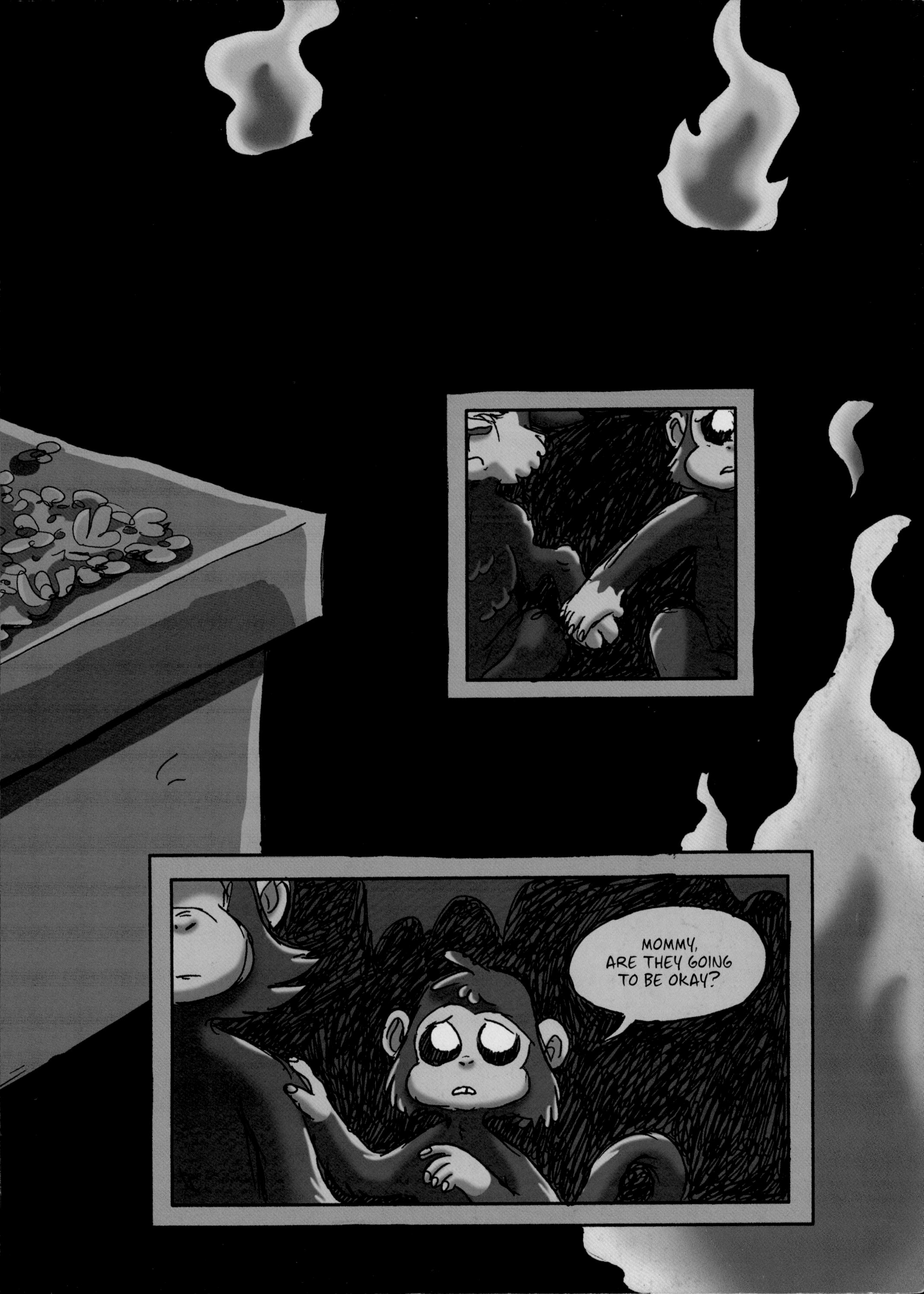
MOMMY, ARE THEY GOING TO BE OKAY?

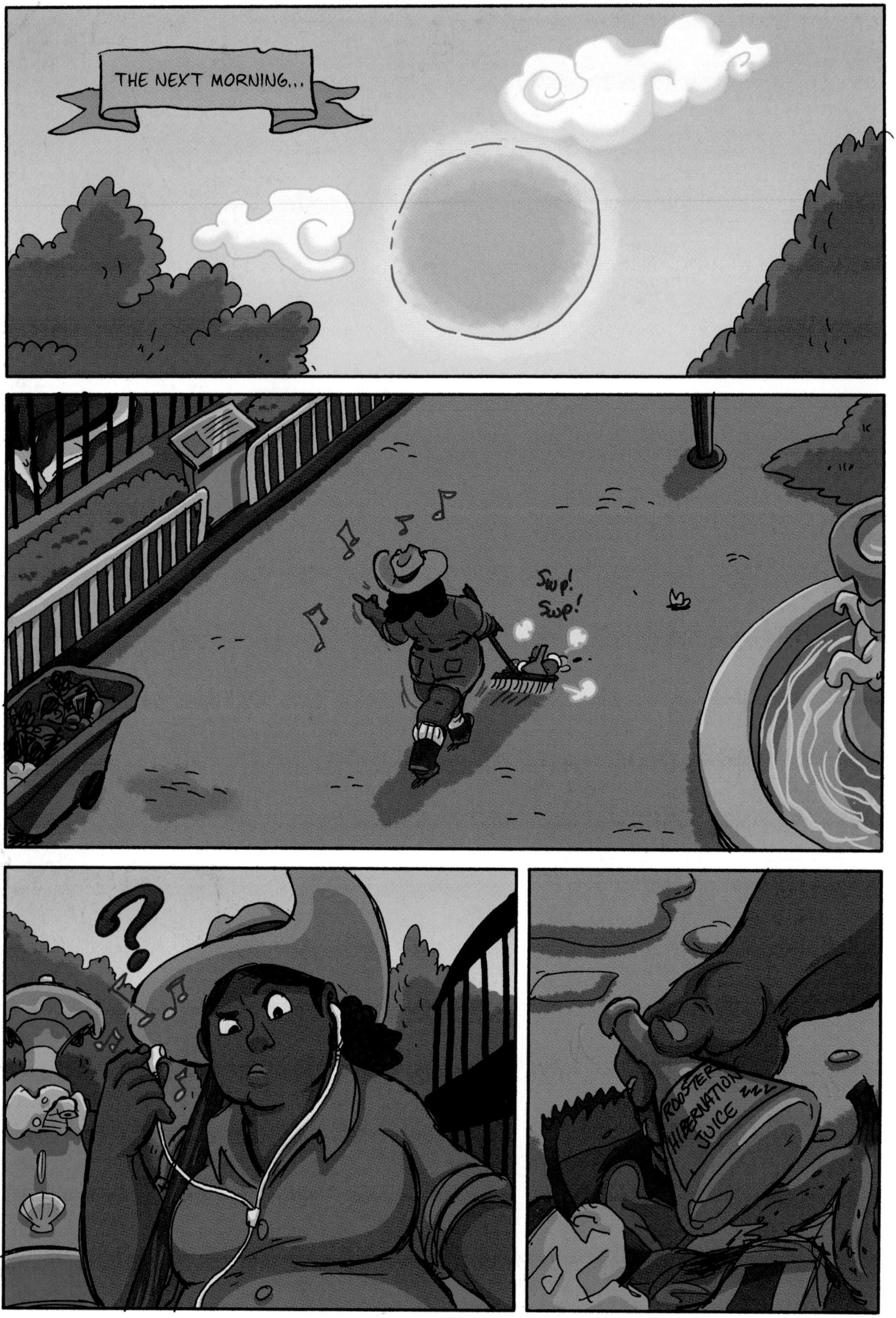
THE NEXT MORNING...
Swp! Swp!
?
ROOSTER HIBERNATION JUICE
ZZZ

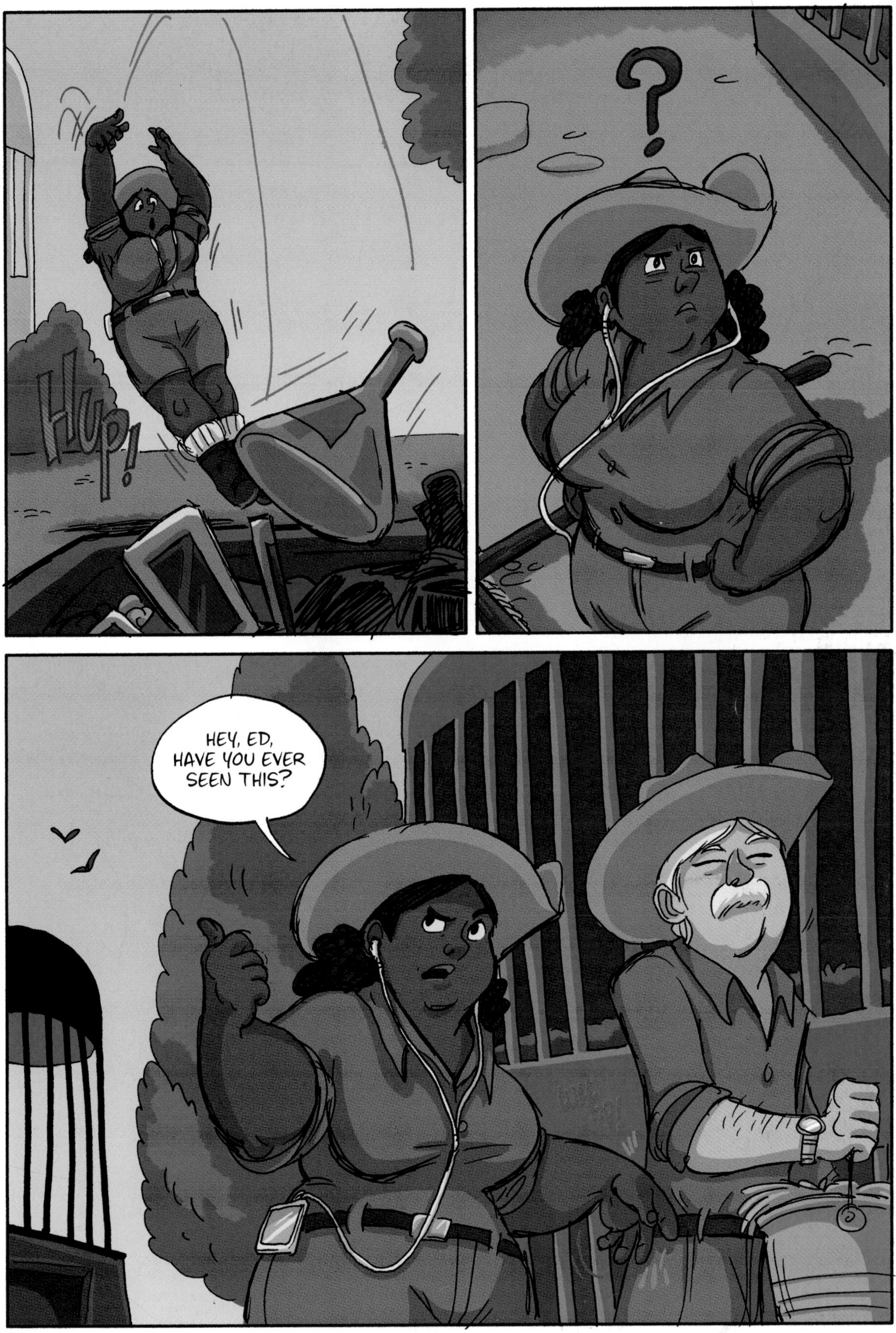
HUP!
?
HEY, ED, HAVE YOU EVER SEEN THIS?

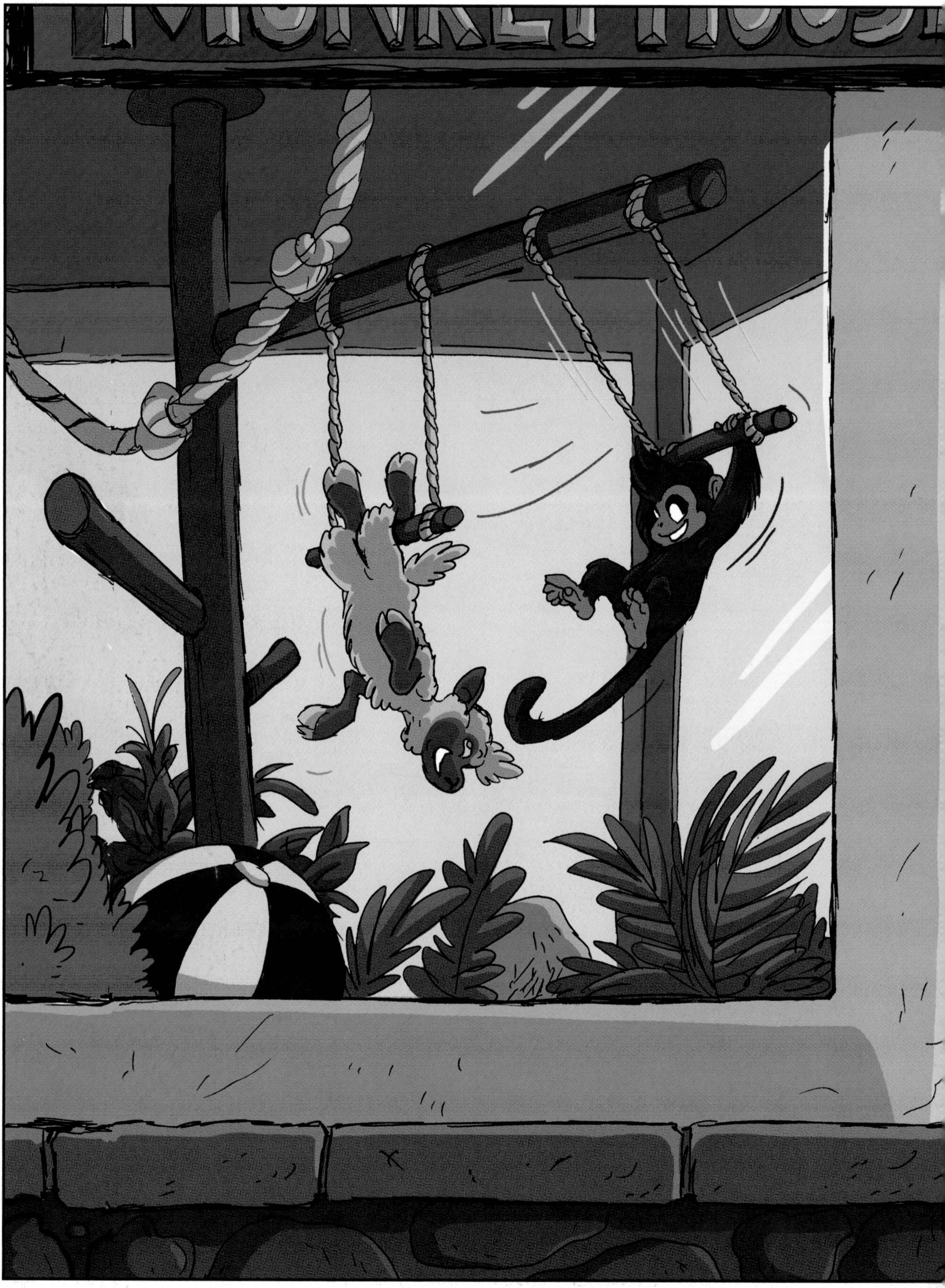

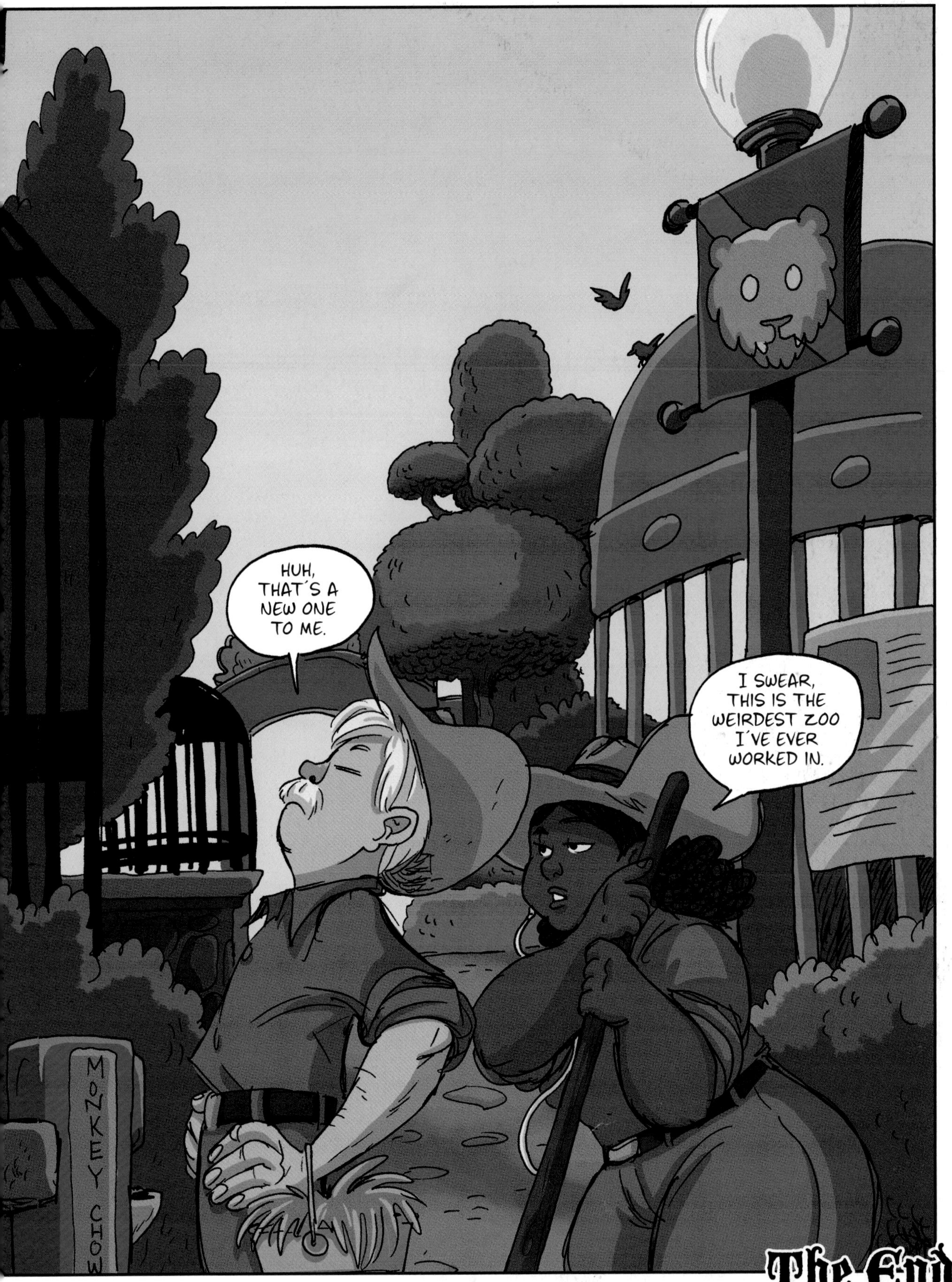
HUH, THAT´S A NEW ONE TO ME.
I SWEAR, THIS IS THE WEIRDEST ZOO I´VE EVER WORKED IN.
MONKEY CHOW
The End

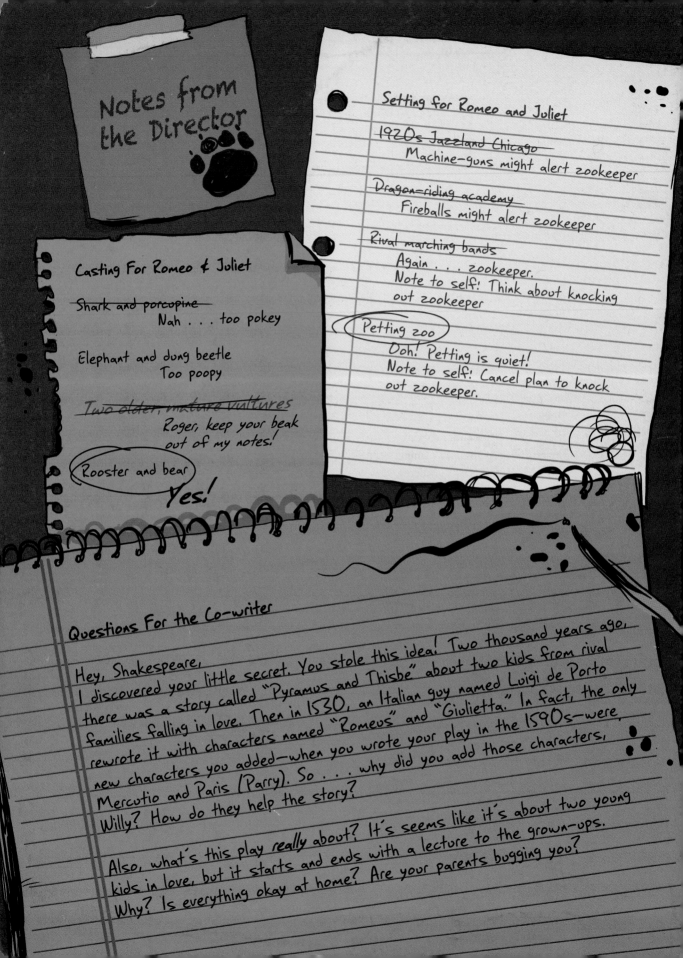

Notes from the Director

Setting for Romeo and Juliet

~~1920s Jazzland Chicago~~
Machine-guns might alert zookeeper

~~Dragon-riding academy~~
Fireballs might alert zookeeper

~~Rival marching bands~~
Again . . . zookeeper.
Note to self! Think about knocking
out zookeeper

(Petting zoo)
Ooh! Petting is quiet!
Note to self! Cancel plan to knock
out zookeeper.

Casting For Romeo & Juliet

~~Shark and porcupine~~
      Nah . . . too pokey

Elephant and dung beetle
      Too poopy

~~Two older, mature vultures~~
      Roger, keep your beak
      out of my notes!

(Rooster and bear)
      Yes!

Questions For the Co-writer

Hey, Shakespeare,
I discovered your little secret. You stole this idea! Two thousand years ago,
there was a story called "Pyramus and Thisbe" about two kids from rival
families falling in love. Then in 1530, an Italian guy named Luigi de Porto
rewrote it with characters named "Romeus" and "Giulietta." In fact, the only
new characters you added—when you wrote your play in the 1590s—were
Mercutio and Paris (Parry). So . . . why did you add those characters,
Willy? How do they help the story?

Also, what's this play *really* about? It's seems like it's about two young
kids in love, but it starts and ends with a lecture to the grown-ups.
Why? Is everything okay at home? Are your parents bugging you?

<u>Notes to Cast and Crew</u>

- I've heard some grumbling from the cast about having to memorize so many lines. Just remember, in Shakespeare's day, actors would perform ten *different* plays every two weeks. So quit complaining!
- Due to the zoo's current lack of bears, Juliet's understudy will be her brother, Reg. This might seem strange, but *Juliet was originally played by a man.* Women weren't even *allowed* on stage until the seventeenth century, over fifty years later.
- After great consideration, I have to deny the cast's request for a cannon. Yes, I understand that Shakespeare used a real cannon in his theater for big entrances and battle scenes, but I feel the zookeeper *might* notice live cannon fire in the middle of the night. Also, those cannons once burned down Shakespeare's entire theater. The zookeeper might notice her entire zoo on fire, too.
- I've decided to cut the twenty minutes of dancing at the end. I know that's how Shakespeare and his actors entertained their audiences after a play, but last week's jig sent three animals to the vet. Some animals were just not meant to cavort. Sorry, hippos. I did appreciate your enthusiasm, though.
- Mercutio and Tibbs: Great energy in the sword-fighting scenes, but it's still a bit sloppy. I want you to rehearse some more tomorrow, for two reasons:

    1) Shakespeare's audience paid to see good fight scenes, so they would boo any actor with poor sword skills.
    2) But more importantly, stage combat is no joke. Actors have lost an eye (or even died!) during sword fights on stage. So your motivation for these scenes is—don't die!

- Some people have asked why we changed a few details from Shakespeare's version. In the original play, the character of the Great Owl (a friar) couldn't contact Romeo and Juliet until it was too late because he was quarantined with the plague. Shakespeare's audience was all too familiar with this. In 1563, the bubonic plague (known as the Black Death) killed over 20,000 people in London alone. That was almost one-third of the city's entire population. And all of this death and disease was *spread by fleas*! I felt that any flea-related plot points would be too scary for our animal audience.

Please Remember:
Check yourself for fleas and ticks after every performance!

To Kusum, of course
—I. L.

For those who draw animals
—Z. G.

First Second

Text copyright © 2015 by Ian Lendler
Art copyright © 2015 by Zack Giallongo

Published by First Second
First Second is an imprint of Roaring Brook Press,
a division of Holtzbrinck Publishing Holdings Limited Partnership
175 Fifth Avenue, New York, New York 10010
All rights reserved

Library of Congress Control Number: 2015937866

Hardcover ISBN 978-1-62672-278-1
Paperback ISBN 978-1-59643-916-0

First Second books may be purchased for business or promotional use. For information
on bulk purchases please contact Macmillan Corporate and Premium Sales Department at
(800) 221-7945 x5442 or by email at specialmarkets@macmillan.com.

First edition 2015
Book design by Colleen AF Venable, Danielle Ceccolini, and John Green

Printed in China by Macmillan Production (Asia) Ltd., Kowloon Bay, Hong Kong (supplier
code 10)

Hardcover: 10 9 8 7 6 5 4 3 2 1
Paperback: 10 9 8 7 6 5 4 3 2 1